## An Hour After Nightfall, You hear Distant Drums. . . .

Their dull, throbbing rhythm sends terror up your spine. They can mean only one thing: The Hukkas are on a death hunt.

For what seems like hours, you track through the dark and dreary marsh.

As you walk, thoughts of the Hukkas ripple through your mind. The Hukkas are the most highly skilled woodsmen and masters of the ambush. Hukka Death is silent: the slashed throat . . . the arrow in the night . . . the screaming, pantherlike attack . . .

Books in the SAGARD THE BARBARIAN GAMEBOOK™ Series
  by Gary Gygax and Flint Dille

#1  THE ICE DRAGON
#2  THE GREEN HYDRA

Available from ARCHWAY paperbacks

HERO'S CHALLENGE™

**SAGARD**

# THE BARBARIAN
GAMEBOOK™

# #2
# THE GREEN
# HYDRA

by Flint Dille and Gary Gygax

**AN ARCHWAY PAPERBACK**
Published by POCKET BOOKS • NEW YORK

AN ARCHWAY PAPERBACK *Original*

 An Archway Paperback published by
POCKET BOOKS, a division of Simon & Schuster, Inc.
1230 Avenue of the Americas, New York, N.Y. 10020

ISBN: 0-671-55488-3

First Archway Paperback printing September, 1985

10 9 8 7 6 5 4 3 2 1

AN ARCHWAY PAPERBACK and colophon are
registered trademarks of Simon & Schuster, Inc.

SAGARD and HERO'S CHALLENGE are trademarks
of Gygax/Dille

Printed in the U.S.A.

IL 7+

# THE GREEN HYDRA

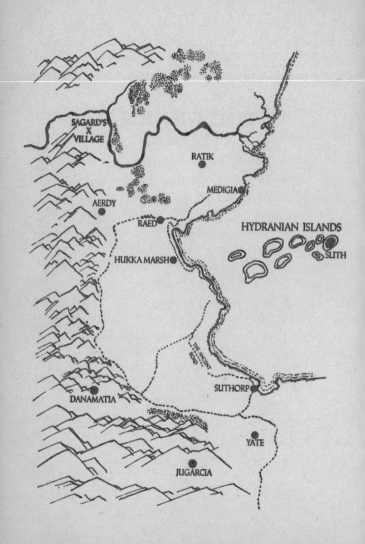

# INTRODUCTION

After his adventure in the lair of the Ice Dragon, the Ratikkan barbarian, Sagard, has become a full warrior in his tribe.

In early spring, he sets out with his tribesmen on a trading mission to the city of Suthorp to exchange furs and pelts for gold pieces.

Crossing through the Southern Marshes, however, they are attacked by Hukkas, and after a furious battle, only Sagard and one Hukka brave remain. Thus begins Book 2,
The Green Hydra . . .

If you have completed Book 1 of the Sagard Series, make a record of the *experience marks* and any *weapons* or *magical items* you gained in the first book and carry them into this book. If you haven't read the first book, start here.

# SECTION 1

A Hukka Warrior, his skin emblazoned with war paint and his feathered spear held high, charges across a murky swamp at you. Holding your *sword*[1] ready, your steel-hewn muscles ache from combat and your heart pounds with rage.

If this is your first Hero's Challenge™ book, turn to Section 102 and read the combat instructions. If not, start the battle. You strike first.

**SAGARD (LEVEL 3: 1/1, 2/1, 3/2, 4/3)**
[20] [19] [18] [17] [16] [15] [14] [13] [12] [11] [10] [9] [8] [7] [6] [5] [4] [3] [2] [1] (Go to Section 3)

**HUKKA WARRIOR (LEVEL 2: 1/0, 2/1, 3/1, 4/2)**
[10] [9] [8] [7] [6] [5] [4] [3] [2] [1] (You have defeated the Hukka Warrior. Go to Section 11.)

If you successfully flee, go to Section 9.

---

1. If you gained a *sword* in the first book, retain the benefits of it. If not, then you are using a regular sword and it will have no effect on combat.

# SECTION 2
## The Escape Stairs

Grasping your plunder, you dash down a short corridor to a flight of stairs which seems to descend forever.

As you dash down the stairs, you hear evenly measured footsteps of Slith Guards, and pick up your pace.

Your flight leads deeper and deeper below the Tomb of the Green Hydra, and as you descend, the stairs grow darker and darker until the portal at the top of the stairs is a dot about the size of a full moon. The deeper you go, the darker it gets until you are in pitch darkness.

In the darkness, your pace slows and you carefully take the steps one at a time. Suddenly, you hit a narrow space of flat flooring and walk a few feet into a pitch-black corridor. Only a few feet down the corridor, you put one foot out and find nothing below it. . . . Losing your balance, you desperately struggle to gain a sound footing, but to no avail and you plummet into a dark void.

Go to Section 89.

# SECTION 3
# Losing to the Hukka Warrior

You lie face down in the swamp. Something is wrong. You should have beaten him easily. Maybe you just had some bad luck. If you are not an experienced challenger, re-read the instructions and try again.

The Hukka is a Level 2 fighter with 10 hit points; you are a Level 3 fighter with *20 hit points*.

**SAGARD (LEVEL 3: 1/1, 2/1, 3/2, 4/3)**
[20] [19] [18] [17] [16] [15] [14] [13] [12] [11] [10] [9] [8] [7] [6] [5] [4] [3] [2] [1] (Begin the book again.)

**HUKKA WARRIOR (LEVEL 2: 1/0, 2/1, 3/1, 4/2)**
[10] [9] [8] [7] [6] [5] [4] [3] [2] [1] (You have defeated the Hukka Warrior. Go to Section 11.)

If you successfully flee, go to Section 9.

# SECTION 4
# Swamp Death

An hour after nightfall, you hear the hollow, malevolent pounding of distant drums. Their dull rhythm sends terror up your spine. Though you do not know the Language of the Drums, you know that they can only mean one thing: The Hukkas are on a death hunt.

Night fog embraces you like velvet as you warily step through the marsh. Though you try to move soundlessly, every footstep through the swamp seems to echo through the murky gloom, and any misstep can bring on Hukka Death.

Hukka Death is quick and brutal: the slashed throat . . . the arrow in the night . . . the screaming, pantherlike attack . . .

Sensing danger, you wheel around and catch a glimpse of a shadowy form slipping behind an ancient, gnarled tree. Out of the corner of your eye, you see another flicker of stealthy activity, and another.

You are surrounded by Hukkas. Go to Section 5.

# SECTION 5
# The Screaming Onslaught

Your nerves burst into flame as the swamp explodes with Hukka war cries. Four Hukkas charge you!

You must fight the quick and fierce Hukka braves. There are four of them of different strengths and endurance levels. You may choose which one to strike each turn. You strike first, then all four Hukkas strike back in rapid succession.

**SAGARD (LEVEL 3: 1/1, 2/1, 3/2, 4/3)**
[20] [19] [18] [17] [16] [15] [14] [13] [12] [11] [10]
[9] [8] [7] [6] [5] [4] [3] [2] [1] (**Begin the book again.**)

**HUKKA #1 (LEVEL 1: 1/0, 2/0, 3/1, 4/1)**
[8] [7] [6] [5] [4] [3] [2] [1]

**HUKKA #2 (LEVEL 2: 1/0, 2/1, 3/1, 4/2)**
[11] [10] [9] [8] [7] [6] [5] [4] [3] [2] [1]

**HUKKA #3 (LEVEL 0: 1/0, 2/0, 3/0, 4/1)**
[20] [19] [18] [17] [16] [15] [14] [13] [12] [11] [10]
[9] [8] [7] [6] [5] [4] [3] [2] [1]

**HUKKA #4 (LEVEL 4: 1/1, 2/2, 3/3, 4/3)**
[5] [4] [3] [2] [1]

When you have defeated all of the Hukkas, go to Section 13.

If you flee, go to Section 46.

# SECTION 6
## The Abandoned Canoe

Not far from the massacre site is an abandoned canoe. Grimly realizing that the Hukkas who stealthily paddled to the ambush will not be needing it anymore, you consider taking it.

It offers you the most expedient mode of travel, *and* perhaps the most dangerous. With it, you can be quickly away from the Hukkas, but you might be visible to owl-eyed Hukkas when the moon comes up.

Shunning the canoe, you may head south by land. By daybreak, you would reach the Ancient Road. The land route, however, has pitfalls of its own, for the Hukkas often lay traps on the marsh-lined trails.

The landward route lies in Section 7.

Take the canoe in Section 35.

# SECTION 7
## Distant Drums

An hour after nightfall, you hear distant drums. Their dull, throbbing rhythm sends terror up your spine. They can only mean one thing, the Hukkas are on a death hunt.

For what seems like hours, you track through the foreboding marsh.

As you walk, thoughts of the Hukkas ripple through your mind. The Hukkas are the most highly skilled woodsmen and masters of the ambush. Hukka Death is silent: the slashed throat . . . the arrow in the night . . . the screaming, panther-like attack . . .

Flip the pages. If the number is even, go to Section 5. If it is odd, go to Section 10.

# SECTION 8
## Slaying the Midnight Horrors

The Nightrippers litter the ground around you. Gain 3 *experience marks*. Gazing out over the forest, you see the eyes of hungry scavengers waiting to devour the spoils of the battle.

Avoiding the hungry predators, you step toward the ancient building, knowing that wild animals are generally loath to enter the dwellings of man.

Entering the ancient structure, you note a strange, unearthly glow surrounding the ancient stones. In the moonlight it is clear that you have entered the ruins of a temple of some long-forgotten religion.

The roof, cracked in the center and letting in a jagged shaft of crystal moonlight, is supported by high, vaulted arches of cut stone. You shudder as you observe that the marble floor is littered with remnants of broken idols of one-eyed gods, multi-armed goddesses, and cloven-hoofed demons.

Stepping over an array of broken columns to an ancient stone cube that sits undisturbed in the center of the structure, you watch the forest.

Go to Section 17.

# SECTION 9
# Fleeing the Hukka Warrior

Your heart pounding, you flee the Hukka Warrior. As your feet splash through the swampy water, you hear him laughing at you.

You should have beaten him easily.

Cowardice is not rewarded in the barbaric realms. If this is your first Hero's Challenge book, you might want to consult the rules again. If not, go back to the beginning of the book and try again.

# SECTION 10
## The Ancient Road

Stepping down the forest path, you come upon a tall fluted column with a pink alabaster bust on top of it. It is nearly impossible to determine how long the stern face atop the pillar has stared blankly off to the horizon or what race he is.

Investigating the site, you discover that a wide road of granite blocks divides the forest. Surely this must be the Ancient Road, which once connected Suthorp to the northern kingdoms. For a long stretch both north and south, it is surrounded on both sides by long rows of broken columns. Once, mighty armies traversed this road, but now it is empty and overgrown.

You follow the road southward and by late day, you can see the jagged towers of Suthorp silhouetted on the horizon like broken teeth. Knowing that bandits often ambush night travelers on this road, you decide to finish your journey in the morning.

You may either pitch your camp in the woods (Section 12), chancing the beasts of the night, or sleep in the ruins of an ancient structure that basks silently in the fading sunlight (Section 14).

# SECTION 11
# Defeating the Hukka Warrior

His spear broken, the Hukka Warrior takes flight through the oozing swamp. Gain *1 experience mark*. You consider chasing him, but you have already fought enough for one day and let him run, knowing that he will soon alert his tribesmen.

All around are the remains of a terrible struggle. The Hukkas ambushed your small trading party, and now their spears stick out of the knee-deep muck like pampas fronds. Hukka shields float in the water along with the tattered remains of your tribesmen.

After dragging the bodies of your people to dry ground, you build a funeral pyre and commend their bodies to flame.

In the flickering firelight, you eat food rations, which will no longer be needed by your comrades, and regain *3 hit points*.

Inspecting the corpses, you discover one that is different from all of the others—not a Hukka at all.

Instead of being covered by bright war paint, this creature, looking more reptilian than human, is clad in black leather armor and his skin is a sickly gray.

On his chest is a *medallion*. Wiping off a layer of slime that covers it, you discover that it is made of glassy volcanic rock and etched with cryptic hieroglyphics which seem to glow as you try to read them. Taking it as a token of the battle, you slip it around your neck. (Note this on your *status chart*.)

Sadness drifts like mist through the darkening swamp. As the sun drops below the horizon, crickets begin their nightly chant and black bats flutter in overhanging trees. And though you try, your mind cannot explain the mysterious gurgling sounds from deep in the brooding gloom.

As darkness covers the sky like a veil of death, you search through a pile of goods you have salvaged. You find several gold and silver trinkets, which will be worth many gold coins to traders in Suthorp. You must make a choice. You may either continue on to Suthorp (see map) or return to your village.

The journey home is in Section 4.

The trek to the city is in Section 6.

# SECTION 12
# The Kingdom of Darkness

In the light of day, men rule the world, but when night falls, other creatures rise from their secret lairs to reclaim it. Snakes slither up from moist grottoes, bears and wolves venture from dens, and other unnamed horrors rise from unholy places to reign over the kingdom of darkness.

As the red sunset drains from the sky like blood from a wound, you build a small fire and cook the last of your food. Regain 5 *hit points*. Leaving the embers glowing, you climb a sturdy branch and drift slowly off to the world of dreams.

In the depth of night when the sky is canopied by brightly glowing stars, you awaken to a soft hooting sound. Opening your eyes, you stare directly into a yellow, glowing eye.

With animal instinct, you lurch back to avoid having your skull crushed in a massive beak. Coming to your senses, you realize that you were very nearly food for a nightripper, a hideous cross between an owl and a bear, five feet tall with rending claws and a crushing beak. Jumping from the tree while ripping your sword from its scabbard in midair, you prepare to do battle with four nightrippers! You strike first.          *(continued on next page)*

**SAGARD (LEVEL 3: 1/1, 2/1, 3/2, 4/3)**
[20] [19] [18] [17] [16] [15] [14] [13] [12] [11] [10]
[9] [8] [7] [6] [5] [4] [3] [2] [1] (You may fight no
more. Begin the book again.)

**NIGHTRIPPER #1 (LEVEL 2: 1/0, 2/1, 3/1, 4/2)**
[9] [8] [7] [6] [5] [4] [3] [2] [1]

**NIGHTRIPPER #2(LEVEL 2: 1/0, 2/1, 3/1, 4/2)**
[8] [7] [6] [5] [4] [3] [2] [1]

**NIGHTRIPPER #3 (LEVEL 1: 1/0, 2/0, 3/1, 4/1)**
[5] [4] [3] [2] [1]

**NIGHTRIPPER #4 (LEVEL 2: 1/0, 2/1, 3/1, 4/2)**
[5] [4] [3] [2] [1]

When you have defeated all of the Nightrippers,
go to Section 8.

If you successfully flee, go to Section 15.

# SECTION 13
# Surviving the Ambush!

Hukkas are scattered throughout the swamp. Gain *3 experience marks*. You remove the jewelry from them and stash them in your pouch, gaining you *many gold pieces* when you get to Suthorp.

As you search the last Hukka corpse for valuables, you once again become conscious of the throbbing of drums to the north, east, and west. Not wanting to chance another encounter, you head to the south—and toward the trading city—knowing that it will be some time before the Hukkas retreat to their secret villages.

Walking all night, you leave the swamp and the Hukkas behind. In the dawn's light, you find yourself in a pleasant, cultivated grove. After eating some fruit, which hangs in abundance from the trees, you lie down and sleep. Regain *12 hit points*.

Go to Section 10.

# SECTION 14
# The Haunted Ruins

As the sun sets, an unearthly glow surrounds the ruins, and though you have not yet entered the building, you cannot vanquish the eerie feeling that something is watching you.

Suddenly, three gray-skinned, lizardlike warriors, brandishing glass scimitars and wearing daggers at their belts, charge you with unnerving silence!

Drawing your sword, you realize that your silent attackers are of the same race as the creature who was dead amongst the Hukka. The name of their horrible race comes to you—Slith!

They could surround you and attack from both sides, but they don't. You sense that they fear the ancient ruins and will not turn their backs on it.

You must fight the Sliths for at least one turn

before fleeing. You attack first, then every Slith attacks you before you attack again.

**SAGARD (LEVEL 3: 1/1, 2/1, 3/2, 4/3)**
[20] [19] [18] [17] [16] [15] [14] [13] [12] [11] [10] [9] [8] [7] [6] [5] [4] [3] [2] [1] **(Begin the book again.)**

**SLITH #1 (LEVEL 2: 1/0, 2/1, 3/1, 4/2)**
[8] [7] [6] [5] [4] [3] [2] [1]

**SLITH #2 (LEVEL 1: 1/0, 2/0, 3/1, 4/1)**
[8] [7] [6] [5] [4] [3] [2] [1]

**SLITH #3 (LEVEL 1: 1/0, 2/0, 3/1, 4/1)**
[8] [7] [6] [5] [4] [3] [2] [1]

When you have defeated all of the Sliths, go to Section 16.

If you successfully flee, go to Section 19.

## SECTION 15
# Flight from the Midnight Horrors

Knowing that you are about to be torn to shreds, you flee the Nightrippers. They give chase, but as you near the ancient structure, they fall behind, stopping a safe distance away.

Taking refuge in the ruins, you note that a strange, unearthly glow surrounds the ancient stones. This was once a temple of a long-forgotten religion.

The cracked roof, supported by high, vaulted arches of sculpted marble, lets in a jagged shaft of crystal moonlight. The floor is littered with remnants of ancient idols: broken one-eyed gods, multiarmed goddesses, and cloven-hoofed demons.

Your heart racing, you search for a safe place in this unnatural edifice.

Stepping over an array of broken columns to an ancient stone cube that lies undisturbed at one end of the ruin, you keep watch, nervously glancing at the statue of a seven-headed dragon with glowing glass eyes. Eyes which look very real. Too real.

Go to Section 17.

# SECTION 16
## Death for the Sliths

As the reptilian Sliths die, their tongues flicker back and forth. Gain 3 *experience marks*. Seeing them lying in the dirt, you notice that each of them wears a glass dagger.

You pick up the three *daggers*. Each one is a perfectly balanced throwing weapon, made of volcanic glass, which has been diabolically hollowed out and filled with poison.

Save the *daggers*. Throwing each one will kill any creature Level 2 or lower, or inflict 3 hit points on any creature above Level 2. These *weapons* are so perfectly made that you can throw two daggers in one combat turn. Mark them on your *status chart*.

Leaving the sliths behind for scavengers, you enter the ancient building. Inside, a strange, unearthly glow surrounds the ancient stones. In the moonlight, which slips through a crack in the roof, you see broken remnants of ancient statues: one-eyed gods, multiarmed goddesses, and cloven-hoofed demons. You have entered what was once a temple of a now-forgotten religion.

Stepping to an ancient stone cube that sits undisturbed in the center of the structure, you keep watch on the forest outside.

Go to Section 17.

# SECTION 17
## Midnight Dreams

As the night passes, dreams merge with reality. The medallion at your chest seems to glow, and you are surrounded by misty spirits. Faces of beautiful priestesses clothed in diaphanous gowns appear before you and chant ancient hymns.

> "For ages we have awaited
> A wandering Ratikkan lad
> To venture boldly onward
> And stop Slith Evil's spread.
>
> Our living breath is stolen
> By undead gray-skinned lords.
> Take courage, mighty warrior,
> Take Ambroth and your sword.

In living tomb of yonder
The chained evil lies.
Wealth and power comes to he
Who smites the Hydra's Eye."

Peach-colored dawn light filters through the ancient structure as you awaken from deep slumber. Looking around, you see no trace of the misty creatures, save for a golden chalice at your feet.

For a moment you eye the cup and the strange glowing liquid inside. It is *Ambroth*, an ancient potion associated with luck. Lifting the cup to your lips, you sip. Strength and *spirit luck* fill your body. Return to *full hit points*.

*Spirit luck* will save you from death. *Once* in the course of battle, you may return to *full hit points* to save yourself. Mark this on your *status chart*.

Go to Section 18.

# SECTION 18
## Trek to Suthorp

Journeying to the city, you contemplate your dream of the night before. You are vexed. You have never heard of the Hydra, but the dream seemed real. And had there been no spirits, there would have been no Ambroth.

By late afternoon, you reach the decaying city of Suthorp. Once Suthorp was a powerful walled city, capital of an important kingdom, but a Davanian invasion has left it a city of broken granite, shattered towers, and crippled men.

Stepping down an elaborate maze of narrow, rubble-strewn cobblestone streets, you are astonished by the great array of people, for you have never been to a city before.

Though destroyed in spirit, the city bustles with commerce. Peasants shuffle down the streets carrying burdens. Young girls sell fruit and dried beef.

Yatian tradesmen in small carts shout as they whip their oxen. Gaudily dressed vixens beckon from alleyways, and tattered beggars, with stumps for arms and legs, beg for alms.

As you have no map, you enlist the aid of an olive-skinned boy from the southern Gyptic deserts to help you for the price of a small Hukka trinket. As you near the shop of Chaga the Trader, the young boy whispers to you, "Chaga is a fair trader; do not refuse his price."

Chaga's shop is dark, dingy, and laden with goods, most of which appear to have been left behind from the war. Battered helmets, scarred swords, and ripped chain mail hang on the wall, while crude goblets and miscellaneous utensils are piled in unsightly heaps about the floor.

At a large table in the center of the shop, several men play games with dice. Upon seeing your mud-spattered garb, they eye you with ill-concealed contempt.

Chaga the Trader, a dun-colored Hitaxian wear-

ing a dust-colored cape and a patch over one eye, sits on a high chair behind a long counter.

"Only one Ratikkan," he says, spotting you. "Usually your tribe sends many men."

"The rest of my party was killed in ambush," you answer. "Though many Hukkas paid with their lives."

"All who kill Hukkas are friends of mine." The Trader turns and snaps his fingers at a young boy. "Bring my friend some Cashka!"

In moments the young boy returns with a small cup of a dark, bitter, sludgelike liquid.

"And what have you for me?" Chaga asks.

Looking warily over your shoulder at the other men in the shop, you pull out a pocketful of jewels that you took from the Hukka.

"You must have killed many Hukkas indeed," he says, studying your jewels. "I will give you one hundred gold pieces."

"They are worth one hundred and fifty," you say.

At this, there is a rustling about the shop. You turn to see all eyes upon you.

"As you are young, I will tell you this once, so listen well: Chaga makes only one offer and that offer is taken."

At this point, you can either take his offer (Section 20), or you can refuse it (Section 22).

# SECTION 19
## Escaping the Sliths

Their mouths dripping foul green saliva and their tongues flicking at you like whips, the Sliths close in.

Desperately hoping to deprive them of victory, you dash toward the crumbling ruins that they seem to fear. Though you hear the flicking of their tongues and their raspy breathing, they do not pursue you. Instead, they throw their jagged glass daggers.

Flip the pages once for each surviving Slith. Lose *3 hit points* for each even number you flip. If you are run down to 0 points, begin the book again. If you survive, keep reading.

You dash into the ancient building. Foiled, they eye you angrily, muttering in a guttural tongue before retreating into the woods.

When it is dark, a strange, unearthly glow surrounds the ancient temple which was once devoted to some now-forgotten religion.

A crack in the center of the roof lets in a jagged shaft of crystal moonlight. On the floor are the broken remnants of ancient statues: one-eyed gods, multiarmed goddesses, and cloven-hoofed demons.

Stepping over broken columns to an ancient stone cube that sits undisturbed in the center of the structure, you keep watch on the forest outside.

Go to Section 17.

# SECTION 20
## The Trader's Price

Heeding Chaga's warning, you sell the jewels at his price.

"You have made a wise decision. There is only one other thing."

"What is that?" you respond.

"I have no gold coins; you must exchange for goods in my shop."

Looking around the shop, you see that all of the items are grossly overpriced. For your one hundred gold pieces, you would only be able to buy a small leather jerkin and a ration kit with food to last you for a few days, with twenty gold pieces left over. While you contemplate, you notice that the other five men in the shop are taking particular interest in your decision.

If you still accept his offer, go to Section 28.

If you change your mind, go to Section 22.

# SECTION 21
# A Straight Fight

With one hand, you give the scroll to the Assassin, while with the other you begin to draw your sword. As he takes the scroll, you jerk the sword from its sheath and attack him.

To see whether surprise is on your side, flip the pages. Even means you attack first, odd means he attacks first. Go to Section 36 to see how you fare in combat against the Slith Assassin.

# SECTION 22
# In Defiance of Chaga's Warning

Indignant, you swoop the jewels into your pocket. As you turn, you hear a low metallic clatter as the men in the shop draw their weapons. You eye them carefully. Though none of them could stand alone against you in combat, there are five of them of all ages and strengths. One is a grizzled Tehnite veteran; another is a tall, olive-skinned Fexian in baggy pants and a conical cap; the third and fourth are both Yatian peasants, one fat, one thin; and the final henchman is a timid but vicious-looking Gyptic—the kind of man who starts fights but flees quickly.

"Slice him," the Gyptic shouts, but none of them moves. As you step toward the door, they move in a circle around you.

"Get him, you lazy brigands, or it's to the street with the lot of you," Chaga calls.

Knowing that you must fight them in order to get out of the shop, you strike first. You may attack them in any order you want.

**SAGARD (LEVEL 3: 1/1, 2/1, 3/2, 4/3)**
[20] [19] [18] [17] [16] [15] [14] [13] [12] [11] [10]
[9] [8] [7] [6] [5] [4] [3] [2] [1] (Begin the book
again.)

**TEHNITE VETERAN (LEVEL 2: 1/0, 2/1, 3/1, 4/2)**
[5] [4] [3] [2] [1]

**FEXIAN (LEVEL 1: 1/0, 2/0, 3/1, 4/1)**
[5] [4] [3] [2] [1]

**FAT YATIAN (LEVEL 1: 1/0, 2/0, 3/1, 4/1)**
[10] [9] [8] [7] [6] [5] [4] [3] [2] [1]

**THIN YATIAN (LEVEL 0: 1/0, 2/0, 3/0, 4/1)**
[15] [14] [13] [12] [11] [10] [9] [8] [7] [6] [5] [4] [3]
[2] [1]

**GYPTIC HENCHMAN (LEVEL 0: 1/0, 2/0, 3/0, 4/1)**
[3] [2] [1]

When you have defeated all of the Trader's
henchmen, go to Section 31.

You may flee only by throwing all of your *jewels*
down so that the men may grovel over them. Lose
all of your *wealth* and go to Section 24.

# SECTION 23
## Duel in the Courtyard

Seizing your best chance, you jump the Slith Assassin. As you drop through the night, he glares up at you with burning eyes.

Flip the pages. If the number you get is even, he can't respond in time and you attack first. If the number is odd, his lightning reflexes allow him to attack first.

Fight for your life in Section 36.

# SECTION 24
# A Costly Escape

Knowing that you cannot win, you dash out of the shop, throwing the *jewels* behind you. The men, whose greed is surpassed by nothing in the realm, forget you and fight each other for the jewels.

For your battle, you are by small degree wiser. Gain *1 experience mark*. Your valuables are gone, but you are still alive.

For the rest of the afternoon, you adopt the disgraceful posture of a beggar to buy a meal. A day of scorn passes, but finally, an old withered woman takes pity on you and drops a single silver coin into your hat.

Proceed, hanging your head, to Section 27.

# SECTION 25
# Greedier Than the Greedy Man

As Chaga begs, the rabble slowly issues in the door like a bucket of thick mud. Paying little attention to them, you put your sword to his throat. "Give me all of your gold and jewels and I *might* spare you, Hitaxian swine!"

Trembling with fear, he pulls a box from behind his desk and you tuck it under your arm. You turn to see the three Tehnite thieves rush toward you. You will have to be *very* lucky to survive this one.

They strike first! You must flip a 1 to flee. If you flee, go to Section 24.

**SAGARD (LEVEL 3: 1/1, 2/1, 3/2, 4/3)**
[20] [19] [18] [17] [16] [15] [14] [13] [12] [11] [10] [9] [8] [7] [6] [5] [4] [3] [2] [1] **(Begin the book again.)**

**TEHNITE THIEVES (LEVEL 3: 1/1, 2/1, 3/2, 4/3)**
   **THIEF #1** [15] [14] [13] [12] [11] [10] [9] [8] [7] [6] [5] [4] [3] [2] [1]

**THIEF #2** [15] [14] [13] [12] [11] [10] [9] [8] [7] [6] [5] [4] [3] [2] [1]

**THIEF #3** [15] [14] [13] [12] [11] [10] [9] [8] [7] [6] [5] [4] [3] [2] [1]

If you defeat the Tehnites, go to Section 26.

# SECTION 26
# Death to the Tehnite Thieves

What you have accomplished is nearly impossible. At this point, check the rules on combat and *make sure* you are correctly using the combat rules, then return to this page.

If you are fighting correctly, then you are now the proud possessor of *1,500 gold pieces.* If you want to continue your adventure, you must hide the gold pieces in the city and come back for them later, then go to Section 27. Or you may end your adventure right now and carry *1,500 gold pieces* into the next book.

Gain *6 experience marks* for your glorious victory.

# 3

# SECTION 27
# Dying Man's Message

A tall stein of Suthorp drink at the Inn of the Merry Wench quenches your thirst (regain *4 hit points*). Through a halo of acrid smoke you watch the night people of Suthorp. Steely-eyed Hitaxian gamblers shake dice . . . laughing Chandanese musicians pluck exotic harps, strum strange instruments, and beat on tropical drums . . . widemouthed braggarts of all races quaff drinks and tell tall tales, while lusty Gyptic dancers perform on thick oak tables.

Your eyes settle on an extraordinary girl atop the minstrel's gallery. She wears a sky-colored gown, and the smoky haze of the inn forms a halo around a cascading river of golden hair. Set high in her perfectly chiseled face are translucent blue eyes which radiate both strength and adventure.

Quickly, you step across the floor of the inn to introduce yourself, but before you can catch her eye, she has vanished like an apparition.

Stepping outside for a breath of fresh air, you hear footsteps. In moments, you hear labored breathing and a fleeing figure painfully shambles up the cobblestone steps. As he draws closer, you see that his face is twisted in a desperate grimace.

Before the grotesque figure reaches you, he drops to the ground. Tossing your drinking glass aside, you rush to the collapsed figure. It is an old man dressed in ornate robes and clutching a scroll in his bent fingers. Blood flows from his mouth, and a glass dagger protrudes from his back.

As you bend down, he speaks to you through bloody lips. "Take this, my son, and give it to Ketza Kota." With surprising strength, he thrusts the scroll into your hand and lets out a loud gasp as his eyes flicker with terrible intensity. "Blessed be you if you succeed; cursed be you if you fail."

His final message delivered, his voice dies, his eyes glaze over and, beyond pain, his head cracks on the cobblestone.

As you close his eyelids you sense the presence of evil and look up. A Slith Assassin, dressed in black, with a face both skeletal and reptilian, stands over you.

From behind shining teeth and a long, vivid reptilian tongue, a raspy voice croaks, "Give me the scroll, Ratikkan fool."

Though you have no intention of letting him keep the scroll, you are of two minds as to how to stop him. You may attack him, hoping to surprise him (go to Section 21), or give him the scroll, in hopes of ambushing him (go to Section 29).

# SECTION 28
# Accepting the Offer

You pause for a moment and hear the rustling of the men in the shop. Out of the corner of your eye, you see one of them reach for his dagger. Discretion is often the better part of valor, and as you are alone in a foreign city, you go along with him.

"I will take your offer," you say.

"A wise decision. For such wisdom, I will give you an extra thirty gold pieces back."

Taking the *leather jerkin*, *ration kit*, and *50 gold pieces*, you leave the shop. Note these items on your *status chart*. The *jerkin* will give you *10 extra damage points* one time in combat, and the *food* will restore 5 *hit points* any time you eat it—but you may not eat it in combat.

Move carefully to Section 27.

# SECTION 29
## Stalking the Assassin

Reluctantly, you hand the scroll to the Slith Assassin.

"You are lucky tonight, Ratikkan dog, for I shall spare you." Then, like a shadow in the night, he vanishes.

Instinctively, you dive to the ground as a dagger whizzes past your ear and smashes on a stone wall behind you, spilling poison that sizzles on the cobblestone.

Leaping to your feet, you set out after the Assassin.

Growing up in Ratikkan forests endowed you with climbing skills which would amaze a city dweller. Thus it is with great ease that you scale the side of the Inn of the Merry Wench. From window ledge to balcony, to rain gutter and finally to the roof, you gain a height advantage on your opponent. Reaching the roof, you spy the Assassin as he makes his way up the torch-lit stone road to his horse, which sits at the far end of the winding lane.

As you carefully make your way across the roof, he turns and looks up toward you. You do not know whether he has seen you or not.

Your first opportunity to jump him comes as he steps through a narrow gate in the middle of the lane. If you want to take this opportunity, go to Section 30. If not, continue reading and await your next chance. If you do not take this chance now, you may not come back to it.

Your second chance comes when he enters a small, open courtyard. As you must pit your sword against his daggers, and swords work best in open areas, you contemplate making the attack here. Not knowing whether you will get an opportunity as good as this again, you must decide whether to jump now. If you do, jump to Section 23. If not, keep reading. You may not come back to this section.

Your final chance comes as the Assassin reaches his horse. In seconds, he will be gone. You must jump him now. Go to Section 32.

# SECTION 30
# Jumping the Slith Assassin

As you descend through the misty night air, the Slith Assassin's yellow eyes flash up at you. With dazzling speed, he ducks. You land on the ground in front of him, barely retaining your balance. With lightning-fast reflexes, he brandishes a dagger and throws it. As the poison-filled dagger flies toward you, duck to Section 36.

He strikes first.

# SECTION 31
# Beating the Trader's Henchmen

The shop is a shambles and littered with moaning henchmen. Gain *4 experience marks*. Angry, you hold your sword to Chaga's throat.

The Trader begs to you, "Spare me." You eye the treacherous Hitaxian icily as he pleads for his life. "I am a rich man. I will give you gold and jewels. You may have anything in my store."

A crowd forms at the door. In it are three large, scarred men who look as strong as you. Looking over their rugged complexions, cold countenances and python vests, you guess that they are serpent-worshiping Tehnites.

You must make a quick decision. You may either grab the nearby leather jerkin and ration kit of Chaga's, keep your money, and let the rabble in, thus giving you time to slip out of the shop, or you may grab for the gold and jewels, risking an encounter with the snake-lovers.

The gold and jewels would come to *1,500 gold pieces,* more than your entire tribe has ever seen.

To take your money, the jerkin, and the food, go to Section 33.

To try for the gold and jewels, go to Section 25.

# SECTION 32
# Jumping Him on His Horse

The Assassin sees you as you drop down toward him, but he is unable to disengage his hands quickly enough to respond. You hack once at him while you fall and once when you land. Therefore, you get two hits before he gets his first one. Waiting for the right time to jump paid off.

Make your hits count in Section 36.

# SECTION 33
# Harsh Justice for Trader Chaga

Worn out from your fight, you call to the rabble whom Chaga has cheated for years. "Take what you want. Chaga wishes to make restitution." The shop floods with beggars and poor men. As you slip out the door, you see the treacherous Trader sink under a surging wave of humanity. Gain *2 experience marks,* for justice is done.

Later, you inspect your new items. They are a *leather jerkin,* a *ration kit,* and *100 gold pieces.* Note these items on your *status chart.*

The *jerkin* will give you *10 extra damage points* one time in combat, and the *food* will gain you 5 *hit points* any time you eat it, except if you are already in combat.

Proceed to Section 27.

# SECTION 34
# The Headless Man and the Talking Head

With your last desperate whack, you decapitate the Slith Assassin. His body still stands, looking as if, even headless, he will continue the fight.

Meanwhile his head rolls across the pavement and settles in a gutter.

"You know not what you are about to do, Ratikkan . . ." a voice says, seemingly from nowhere.

You spin around, looking for the speaker, but there is none. Then you realize that the severed head itself is speaking. "For this, you shall suffer the death of a million cuts."

As you watch in horror, the red tongue stops wagging and the Assassin's body collapses to the pavement.

With a shudder, Gain *3 experience marks*.

Go to Section 40.

# SECTION 35
## Taking the River

The canoe drifts slowly through an eerie swamp filled with twisted trees and curtains of moss that hang like waiting serpents. The darkening sky is aswirl with bats, and from the distant woods comes the glimmer of hungry, glowing eyes.

Stilling your breath, you paddle softly, knowing that the slightest sound could bring a teeming flock of Hukka arrows. Regain 5 *hit points.*

In time, the throbbing of distant drums begins. At first, you only hear them to the west, but gradually, the haunting rhythms come from all sides.

Their hollow, monotonous beat sends terror up your spine. The drums can only mean one thing: The Hukkas are on a death hunt!

You hear intermittent rustling sounds from the shore, but you see nothing. Your muscles scream for a rest, but still you summon the strength to paddle harder.

As you watch for motion in the woods, a woman's voice calls to you out of the darkness. "Come, brave warrior! Let me heal your pains."

Looking to the far bank, you see a shapely form silhouetted in the moonlight. Curious, you start to turn the canoe when a sudden jolt throws you forward. In the instant before the canoe tips, you see what appears to be a large log in the dark, murky water. Suddenly, the "log" seems to split in half, revealing two long rows of blade-sharp teeth!

Desperately, you dive from the canoe as a monstrous mouth crushes the front half of your canoe!

You dip under the dark, slimy water. Terror fills your heart as you brush against the scales of a hideous beast.

Rising to the top, you hear a bestial hiss and look up in horror. A hideous creature is silhouetted against the full moon. It stands ten feet fall and has the body of a dinosaur with the head of a crocodile. It is called a Crocosaurus.

Armed with sharp claws and pulverizing jaws, the Crocosaurus is a formidable enemy. Its only weakness is that it is slow. Were you on dry land, you might be able to flee from it, but you are knee-deep in swamp.

Because of your speed, you *strike twice* for each time he strikes you.

SAGARD (LEVEL 3: 1/1, 2/1, 3/2, 4/3)
[20] [19] [18] [17] [16] [15] [14] [13] [12] [11]
[10] [9] [8] [7] [6] [5] [4] [3] [2] [1] (Begin the book
again.)

CROCOSAURUS (LEVEL 5: 1/2, 2/3, 3/3, 4/4)
[25] [24] [23] [22] [21] [20] [19] [18] [17] [16]
[15] [14] [13] [12] [11] [10] [9] [8] [7] [6] [5]
[4] [3] [2] [1]

If you kill the Crocosaurus, go to Section 43.

To flee the Crocosaurus, you must flip an even
number, and as you flee, he strikes at you once. If
you successfully flee, go to Section 41.

# SECTION 36
# Battling the Slith Assassin

Never before have you fought so highly trained a killer. The Level of the Assassin's fighting ability goes down with the number of hit points he has remaining. From 25 to 21 he is Level 5, From 20 to 16 he is Level 4, from 15 to 10 he is Level 3, from 9 to 5 he is Level 2, and 4 and below he is Level 1. It is in your interest to do as much damage as you can quickly.

**SAGARD (LEVEL 3: 1/1, 2/1, 3/2, 4/3)**
[20] [19] [18] [17] [16] [15] [14] [13] [12] [11]
[10] [9] [8] [7] [6] [5] [4] [3] [2] [1] (**Begin again.**)

**THE SLITH ASSASSIN**
   **(LEVEL 5: 1/2, 2/3, 3/3, 4/4)**
[25] [24] [23] [22] [21]
   **(LEVEL 4: 1/1, 2/2, 3/3, 4/3)**
[20] [19] [18] [17] [16]
   **(LEVEL 3: 1/1, 2/1, 3/2, 4/3)**
[15] [14] [13] [12] [11] [10]
   **(LEVEL 2: 1/0, 2/1, 3/1, 4/2)**
[9] [8] [7] [6] [5]
   **(LEVEL 1: 1/0, 2/0, 3/1, 4/1)**
[4] [3] [2] [1]


When you defeat him, go to Section 34.
You may *not* flee the Slith Assassin.

# SECTION 37
## Midnight in the Swamp

The withered hag sends cold shivers up your spine, so you cross the swamp on the far bank. As you reach the opposite shore, you turn and glance nervously over your shoulder. For a moment in the moonlight, she looks young and beautiful. You can still go back and meet her if you want to (go to Section 39); if not, keep reading.

Heading deep into the swamp, you find a small pool teeming with fish. You skewer one of them with your sword, then build a small fire and eat. Regain 6 *hit points*.

Go to Section 47.

# SECTION 38
## Midnight Rendezvous

As watchmen shout curfew on the sleeping streets, you creep to the appointed rendezvous.

From the shadows of an arched doorway you keep lookout on the enormous statue of Garagus Rex. As the church bell strikes midnight, a glowing form drifts silently down the street and stops under the towering statue.

Creeping silently toward the figure, and recognizing that it is a girlish form, you whisper to her. "I am here."

"Not a moment too soon," she says. "For we are pursued by spies. Follow me to the tower, but do not get too close."

You follow her to a broken and abandoned tower within sight of the statue. When you reach the chilly, damp remnant of Suthorp's era as a great power, you look back to see that another form waits near the statue of Garagus Rex, and your skin crawls.

Wheeling around, you realize that you are not in the company of a woman but of a demon!

The girlish shape makes a remarkable transformation. It doubles in size and wields a massive battle-ax. This is the Smoke Demon, spawned in the depths of the underworld to do the dark bidding of evil.

Before you can respond, the Smoke Demon snatches the map from your hand. You must have the map. In order to get it, you have no choice but to fight the Smoke Demon.

Before each round of combat, flip to see if you

can steal the map back (flipping 1 gets it back). If you do get it back, flee in the normal manner, because the Smoke Demon cannot be defeated. When you hit him, his form, made of smoke, reassembles.

The Smoke Demon is a Level 3 (1/1, 2/1, 3/2, 4/3) fighter. He fights each turn after you flip for the map or flip to flee. You may *not* flee without the map.

SAGARD (LEVEL 3: 1/1, 2/1, 3/2, 4/3)
[20] [19] [18] [17] [16] [15] [14] [13] [12] [11]
[10] [9] [8] [7] [6] [5] [4] [3] [2] [1] (Begin the book again.)

Flee with map to Section 44.

# SECTION 39
# The Swamp Woman

Your senses alerted, you step toward the witchy hag. As you reach her, she motions for you to follow her, and you do, your sword drawn.

Several hundred yards along a muddy path, you come upon her shed, fashioned of many small trees all bent to form a roof and walls.

Carefully, you enter the sparsely furnished hut. "For generations, the Crocosaurus has preyed upon all who come into this part of the woods. Even the Hukkas yield this place to him. Only I escaped its wrath because it used me as bait. I could not count the number of men I have lured to their death on this river over the centuries." She laughs strangely. "For, though it is hard to believe, this wrinkled face was once young and beautiful."

As she speaks, she rubs you with an ointment, and your pain subsides. As you heal, your eyes grow heavy. The gates of sleep begin to swing closed, and the ravages of time melt from the hag's face. A decade recedes each minute, until she becomes the young and beautiful vision you saw on the shore.

As you reach for her, she lifts her hand to your

eyes and says, "Sleep for now, Ratikkan," and she lowers your eyelids.

You fall into a deep sleep. Regain *all* your *hit points.*

When you awake in the morning she is gone. On the floor is a shiny coin and near it, in delicate handwriting, is a note: "Follow the trail of coins and you shall have your path away from here."

Picking up the coin, you gaze out of the strange house and see yet another coin shining on the trail far away. Picking up the second coin, you see yet a third, much farther down the trail.

All the day long, you follow the trail of coins. It leads through shrouded paths of incredible beauty where spring plants flourish under waterfalls and across the branches of mighty trees.

Each time you think you have lost the path, another coin is caught by the sunlight and leads you on. Finally, when you reach what turns out to be the last coin, you find a note: "Follow the setting sun and you shall find the Ancient Road. The Hukkas will bother you no more. One day, Ratikkan, we shall meet again—Marianta."

Your heart flutters as you remember the stunning beauty that stared down at you as you drifted to sleep. "Yes, one day we shall meet again," you say.

Head to Section 10.

# SECTION 40
# Defeating the Slith Assassin

The Slith Assassin lies dead on the stone street. Gain *4 experience marks*. Rifling his pockets, you find 27 *gold pieces* and a small piece of paper with two words on it—KETZA KOTA.

Seeing that a small crowd has gathered around the corpse, and not wanting to gather any more attention than necessary, you quickly walk to a small inn near the edge of town.

You are in your room for two minutes when you fall fast asleep on a bed of soft down.

You awaken with a start to see the mistress of the inn. "Excuse me, sir, but I thought you should have something to eat," a voice says. "You have been asleep for two days." Regain *all* your *hit points*.

Slowly waking up, you look for the scroll. It is missing! For nearly an hour you turn the room upside down but to no avail. Finally, though, you discover that you slept on it. Unrolling it, you take your first look.

Not knowing the alien language on the map, you can only speculate its meaning. It must be a map to something of great importance—a temple, a palace, a tomb—something.

You know of at least one man who died clutching

this map, and given that a Slith Assassin was set on his trail, you grimly realize that you, too, are probably being stalked.

Knowing it will not be long before they find you, you must take action. You can try to find the mysterious Ketza Kota (search in Section 42).

Or you can attempt to break the coded message (then go to the Section mentioned in the code.)

Or you can take the map to a Priest of Maji Mahot, a dying sect that studies strange languages and ancient lore, at Section 97.

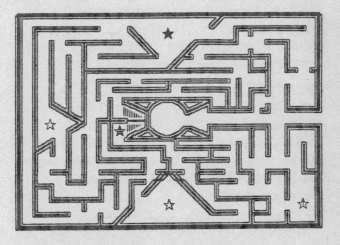

# SECTION 41
# Fleeing the Crocosaurus

Dripping with blood, you turn and flee the hideous creature. As he pursues you, you feel his cold, slimy breath spattering your back.

Reaching the shore, you see the beautiful woman who lured you onto this shore transform into a bent hag who cackles at you through black gums and broken teeth.

Through the night, you run through the oozing swamp, gashing and bruising yourself on sharp plants and jutting branches. Blood seems to flow from every pore of your body. Finally, darkness overtakes you and you stumble to the ground.

Awakening in the morning, you find that you are in a lush orchard. In the trees overhead, you see a tall tree with a hut perched in it. As hunger gnaws at your belly, you reach into a tree and pull a fruit from it. Regain *10 hit points.*

All day, you trek through the pathless swamp, hopelessly lost. As the sun goes down, you set out for the west, hoping somehow to connect with the Ancient Road.

Walk carefully to Section 47.

# SECTION 42
## In Search of Ketza Kota

The lobby of the inn is a small, squat, cheerless room with a counter, a couple of uncomfortable chairs, a large hearth, and a curtained doorway leading, you presume, to the kitchen.

The slender, nervous innkeeper eyes you suspiciously as you pay for your stay.

"I am in search of a man known as Ketza Kota," you say, breaking the awkward silence.

"I know of no such man," the innkeeper responds, not looking up from the papers that sit on his desk. Looking over his shoulder, you catch sight of a tall, thin form listening at the curtained doorway.

Before you can rip the curtain open to see who is eavesdropping on you, the misty shape vanishes and small puffs of smoke drift through the curtain. Sensing dark magic, you step outside to the sundrenched streets of Suthorp.

A bright spring sun warms the bustling city, and the scent of newly cut flowers wafts through the air. Across the narrow street from the inn, the extraordinarily beautiful woman from the pub tends a flower cart. Before you can make a move in her direction, she turns and steps quickly toward you, almost as if she were waiting for you.

"Flowers for your love?" she asks.

"I have no love," you respond.

"Perhaps the flowers shall help you to find one," she says, holding forth a bouquet of roses. Then, drawing very close to you, she says, "I can lead you to Ketza Kota."

You answer only with a stunned gaze. How could she know you are looking for Ketza Kota?

She answers your unasked question. "Secrets are scarce in Suthorp." Then, looking around to be sure she isn't overheard, the beautiful girl quickly whispers. "Convene with me at the statue of Garagus Rex at midnight—we are being watched."

Before you can respond, she hurries over to another customer.

Looking over your shoulder, you see a misty figure watching from a darkened window of the inn, and a chill runs down your spine.

You spend the day on the streets of Suthorp. In the course of an endless journey through winding alleys, you pass nearly a hundred market stalls filled with fruit, leather goods, and trinkets from distant lands, and watch with mild amusement as a pickpocket protests his innocence from the pillory.

In the late afternoon, passing through the guild hall you spy the misty silhouette watching you from the shadowy belfry of the church.

Go to Section 38.

# SECTION 43
# Beating the Crocosaurus

The Crocosaurus floats lifelessly, its evil reptilian eyes staring at the moon and its claws twitching. Gain *4 experience marks*.

Washing your blade, you become aware of the bent figure of an old woman holding a lantern and watching you from the shore.

"Come, my lad. I shall wash your wounds."

If you want to trust the woman, go to Section 39.

If you do not want to trust the woman, go to Section 37.

# SECTION 44
# Fleeing with the Map

Holding the map tightly, you dash out of the tower toward the statue of Garagus Rex. The Smoke Demon pursues you, drifting more than running, and flailing his devilish ax.

As the Smoke Demon gains on you, the figure under the statue raises a large jewel which emits a blinding flash of light that ignites the street.

The Smoke Demon lets out a thundering roar as a screaming whirlwind rips the street, blowing you off your feet like a leaf.

A torrent of destruction rages. Signs are torn from their braces, windows are sucked from the frames, and flowerpots shatter on the street. The colossal statue, caught in the cyclone, spins on its base, teeters, and tumbles into a stone building, falling to the ground with a mighty crash.

High above you, the Smoke Demon dissipates in a tornado of agony.

As quickly as it came, the wind dies down and the Smoke Demon is gone. The flower girl, holding the jewel, stands alone under the statue.

She casts away the jewel, its powers spent, and steps toward you.

"Are you all right?" she asks.

"I'm all right, but Garagus Rex has seen better days," you say, eyeing the statue's feet, which protrude from a pile of wreckage.

"Follow me quickly," she says, and turns away.

You follow her through a network of twisting streets to a shabby little garret in the shadows of Suthorp's north wall. Drawing a silver key from her sleeve, she opens the door.

Once in the apartment, she unfurls a great tapestry and covers the window. Without so much as lighting a candle, the beautiful creature slides a faded Hitaxian rug away from its place on the floor, revealing a trap door.

Lifting the door reveals a stairway. Lighting a long taper, she leads you down. Stepping off the stairs, she lights several wall torches shedding light on a large vaulted chamber.

"A thousand years ago this was the dungeon of Garagus Rex," she says. "After he died and the city was burned, this caldron of horror was forgotten."

Leading you to a stone slab which is stained red and was probably once used for beheadings, she puts a graceful hand out. "May I have the map?" she asks.

"I am to give it to Ketza Kota."

She looks at you directly, a blue flame glowing in her eyes. "I am Ketza Kota!"

You are stunned. You had expected a wizened old sorcerer, and are now amazed to discover that she is a stunning young woman. You hand her the map.

"Behold the Tomb of the Green Hydra," she says, carefully unrolling it on the stone block. "The old man who gave it to you was its architect. While he was building it, he discovered that his employers were planning to kill him on completion. Thus, he designed a secret escape passage and slipped away. The assassins pursued him over water and land."

"I know the rest of the story," you say, remembering the dying man and the Slith Assassin. "But why was he bringing it to you?"

"Because I offered shelter in exchange for the map."

"But why? What is in the tomb?" you ask. "Treasure?"

"I am no treasure seeker," she says. "I am one who wishes to destroy the Green Hydra."

"But it is dead—why else would they build a tomb for it?"

"It is far from dead. Rather, it is in a dulled stupor. As long as it lives, Slith Evil will spread."

"Sliths!" you exclaim. "Everywhere I go, I encounter them."

With firelight flickering off her features, she tells the tale of the Green Hydra. "The Sliths," she says, "are both the captors and captives of the Green Hydra.

"For five hundred years, the Green Hydra ravaged the Isle of Slith, feeding upon human flesh. Though the men of Slith wanted to kill it, legend has it that if the Hydra were killed, a demon would rise up from each of its severed heads to ravage the Isle.

"In an effort to placate the monster, the Sliths fed humans to the beast. One woman, Rotanna, whose beauty was matched only by her brilliance, begot a plan to subdue the Hydra. Before she was sacrificed, she ate a great quantity of the Night Dahlia, which contained a powerful and deadly sleep potion. Thus, when the Hydra devoured her it fell into a deep sleep.

"The Sliths then ventured to keep the Hydra forever asleep, thus stopping it from killing, yet keeping the demons pent up inside it.

"Each time the Hydra began to stir, they shot it with an arrow covered with the resin of the Night Dahlia, returning it to slumber. It was not long before most of the island's crops were given up to grow Night Dahlia. However, the presence of the mind-altering plant made the Sliths become dark and evil. Thus, the Sliths, who were once good, are now evil slaves to the Dahlia."

She stops for a moment to take a breath. "There is another reason for the spread of Slith Evil. Each day, it takes more Night Dahlia to keep the Hydra subdued. Though they grow a great deal, they have to buy Dahlia from the Hitaxians at high prices. To pay for it, they steal from others. But even so, the Hydra might escape any day." She pauses as though she has come to the end of her story.

"But you still haven't told me about the tomb," you say.

"Well, the Hydra has many dark and demonic allies who have tried to release her. To prevent this, the Sliths enclosed her in the tomb to keep the demons out. . . ."

You nod. "And what do you hope to do?"

"Kill the Hydra and release the demons. They shall purge the Isle and, in time, they will destroy each other, thus cleansing the Isle." The firelight catches a fierce intensity in her eyes as she speaks. "I am a Slith who has not been corrupted by the Night Dahlia."

"I wish you luck, but for now I had best be going," you say, beginning to suspect what she is after.

She looks deeply into your eyes. "I am not a warrior. A warrior must carry out this task. Please, Sagard, I beg you. Only someone of your strength could kill the Hydra."

"And not live to tell of it . . ." you respond.

Ketza Kota tries every known means to persuade you. She tells you of treasures that might be yours, of the great heroism you will achieve, but in the end it is her beauty that persuades you.

"I will do it," you finally say, regretting the words as they slip out of your mouth. The beautiful girl throws her arms around you and hugs you, setting your heart to pounding harder than any beast has.

As you catch your breath, she turns her attention to the map. For a long time, she moves her pen around and finally, with a laugh, declares that she has broken the code.

"You must enter the first chamber to take arrows. In the second chamber, you will find essence of the Dahlia; and in the third chamber, you will find the Hydra. Render her unconscious with the arrows and slay her. Then, be gone through the secret chamber before the demons arise."

Eyeing the plan and remembering the deadly Sliths you have already encountered, you look up at her. "Is there nobody else to do this?"

"I guess I should tell you. A month ago we hired an Aerdian Mercenary, armed with fire darts, to go to the island. He never returned."

A pit grows in your stomach, but steeling your courage, you respond. "I shall be more successful."

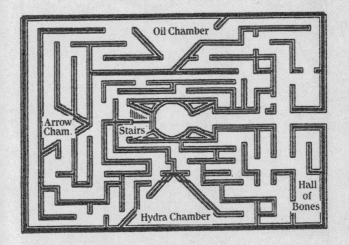

Oil Chamber

Arrow Cham.

Stairs

Hall of Bones

Hydra Chamber

**High Priestess Ketza Kota,**

This note is written in haste. There is but one way to destroy the Green Hydra and survive. Enter the Arrow Chamber and take the arrows. Then proceed to the Oil Chamber and dip the arrows in Dahlia Oil. From there, proceed directly to the Hydra Chamber, shoot the arrows and cut off the Hydra's head. Escape through the secret stairs.

Trust nobody in the Tomb of the Green Hydra. It is possible that there are flame darts on the corpse of an adventurer in the Hall of Bones. These are powerful weapons.

Go to Section Forty-five.

Ketza Kota looks up at you. "Be cautious, **Sagard**, and take this with you."

She steps across the vaulted room and opens an enormous trunk. In it is a beautiful, finely linked *chain-mail shirt*. The shirt will serve you well, for you can deduct 1 hit point from every hit. For example, if you are hit for 3 points, mark off only 2; and if you are hit for 1 point, take no damage. Note this on your *status chart*.

Go to Section 45.

# SECTION 45
# The Docks

The pink dawn light is broken in segments by the lines of tall masts, and tinted by brightly dyed sails adorned with strange and powerful creatures: dragons, eagles, and snakes.

As the sun rises on the horizon, the docks bustle with activity. Merchants, fishermen, travelers, and even white-haired, red-eyed Vulzar raiders, make ready their ships.

Peering into the water, you see a most peculiar sight: A man, human in all ways except for his scaled legs, wearing ornate and shiny robes, rides a huge whiskered fish.

A chill shakes you as you spy an enormous trireme flying a black sail emblazoned with a death's head, for any schoolboy knows it belongs to

Salamar Rabfahd, a Hitaxian pirate who would just as soon slash your throat as look at you.

Stepping up to an old salt who is carefully laying out his nets for a day of fishing, you ask him for transport to the Isle of Slith.

"You won't get me near that island for all the money in Suthorp."

"Who will go to it?"

He holds out a hand and, after you have filled it with a coin, responds. "Only Swarny Pate would sail in those waters, and he is not to be trusted."

Swarny Pate's boat is the ugliest in the harbor— all gray, in need of maintenance, and smelling of rotted fish and filth. Stepping onto his ship, you encounter his two crewmen, who appear to be Fexians with lean, mean muscles, crimson lips, and cold, hungry black eyes. After hearing your request, they sullenly lead you into Swarny Pate's cabin.

In the cabin, which is littered with various maps and charts and the bloody remains of fish, sits Swarny Pate. He is a cold, rutted character with reddish skin, many times burned by the sun, a gouged black hole where one eye should be, and broken teeth. On one shoulder sits a Lizrot, an ugly flying bird/lizard with a long, licking tongue and sharp claws.

"I will take you to the Isle of Slith—for fifty gold pieces. I will return you for the same price. Take it or leave it."

Having no other option, you take his offer. "I will give you twenty-five in advance, and seventy-five upon return."

He nods in agreement and in less than an hour you set sail. As you do not trust the crew, you stand at the back of the ship silently watching them. Occasionally, you notice them glance stealthily up at you, trying to see if you are watching them, but for the most part, they pilot the ship. You know, however, that should your attention slip for only a moment, they may jump you.

When night comes, you are extremely suspicious and take pains not to drift off to sleep, for there is no doubt in your mind that falling asleep would lead you to a watery grave with your gold coins in their scurvy hands.

Check your hit points.

If you have more than 10 points, flip the pages. If you get an even number, go to Section 101. If you get an odd number go to Section 99.

If you have 10 hit points or fewer, go to Section 99.

# SECTION 46
# Fleeing the Hukkas

A Hukka ax whizzes over your head. Knowing that you are about to die, you raise your sword to inflict as much damage on them as you can.

Suddenly, you hear a loud growl and turn to see an enormous tiger stalking toward you. The Hukkas step back, taking defensive positions, while you dash toward the river.

In the instant you dive for the water, you see the tiger jump at the Hukkas. Fate has intervened to save you this time, but don't expect it to happen again.

Surfacing several hundred feet away from the tiger and the Hukkas, you hear Hukka screams and feline growls. Taking advantage of the diversion, you swim farther down the river.

Cut, tired, and aching from your battle, you step onto the river bank and survey the river for fish.

Spotting a large trout, you skewer it on the end of your sword and retreat into the woods to eat it.

When you are done, you climb to a large branch and fall asleep. Regain 9 *hit points* and *1 experience mark*.

When you awaken, it is dark, but the moon is full and provides a lighted path through the forest.

Go to Section 47.

# SECTION 47
# The Burial Mound

Late at night you discover a large clearing. In the center of the clearing stands an unnatural mound, nearly fifteen feet high. Ringing the mound are tall stakes topped with bleached skulls of animals and men. The manmade hill could only have one identity—it is a Hukka burial mound!

A civilized man would shudder at the sight of a burial mound, but you are not civilized. The Hukkas have brutally slaughtered many of your tribesmen. Knowing that Hukkas bury treasures with their dead, you head to the top of the mound to pilfer the jewels within.

Your heavily muscled legs carry you to the top of the mound in seconds. Looking around, you see no hint of Hukkas, and the forest is strangely quiet. Using your sword as a shovel to loosen the dirt, you begin digging. The night grows long as you dig deep into the mound.

Stopping to rest, you hear sounds from above. At first, you think it is the wind, but straining your ears, you realize it is the sound of voices—voices chanting in the Hukka tongue.

Cold terror grips you. You are at the bottom of a hole and there is nowhere to run. You are trapped!

Two possible courses of action enter your mind. Either climb to the top of the hole and attack (go to Section 57), or hide at the bottom of the hole (go to Section 71).


# SECTION 48
## The Berard

A hideous claw tears at your flesh. Take *3 hit points* no matter what kind of armor you have. Before you can fight back, the demonic beast, who moves very slowly, drops you into a sticky puddle of filth. You must fight this monster if you hope to survive. You may flee only if you flip a 4. If you flee, return to the map at Section C and keep moving.

You strike first.

**SAGARD (LEVEL 3: 1/1, 2/1, 3/2, 4/3)**
[20] [19] [18] [17] [16] [15] [14] [13] [12] [11] [10]
[9] [8] [7] [6] [5] [4] [3] [2] [1] (Begin the book again.)

**BERARD (LEVEL 5: 1/2, 2/3, 3/3, 4/4)**
[29] [28] [27] [26] [25] [24] [23] [22] [21] [20] [19]
[18] [17] [16] [15] [14] [13] [12] [11] [10] [9] [8] [7]
[6] [5] [4] [3] [2] [1] (He is defeated. Return to the map, gaining *3 experience marks*.)

# SECTION 49
# Running the Gamut

Hoping for more jewels, you await the arrival of the Hukka braves and priests. As they draw closer, you realize that the line consists of twenty Hukka braves and two Hukka priests. Your heart pounds. No longer are you simply fooling a bunch of old men, women, and children, but you will have to stare eye to eye with Hukka priests.

You have one last chance to flee (go directly to Section 50 without reading further).

When the Hukkas arrive, the priests step toward you and eye you quizzically, then speak to each other in hushed tones. Trying to act like a Hukka ghost, you stare sullenly off into the distance. However, you cannot help but see the glint of an enormous golden trunk which has been brought in offering and your imagination swirls with visions of the shining jewels that might be in the chest.

Their secret conference finished, the Hukka priests address you in an ancient tongue. Not knowing their language, you sit in silence. This greatly impresses the braves, but disturbs the priests.

Again, they try to address you, and again you are mute. Dissension ripples through the band of Hukkas. Though you do not speak their language, it is not hard to understand what is happening. The priests are not getting the response from you they expect and their tribesmen are losing faith in them.

As the tension grows, you make no motion,

though your heart pounds. In desperation, one of the priests points to you and shrieks something in Hukka. He then charges you, his dagger drawn. You jump up, brandishing your sword as the second priest joins the attack. You must fight the Hukka priests. They are Level 0 fighters, and only have 5 hit points. However, if they manage to inflict even 1 hit point on you, they have proved that you are a fraud, in which case, run for your life to Section 65. If you take no damage, go to Section 52.

You may *not* flee the Hukka priests.

**SAGARD (LEVEL 3: 1/1, 2/1, 3/2, 4/3)**
**(If you take a single hit point, go to Section 65.)**

**HUKKA PRIESTS (LEVEL 0: 1/0, 2/0, 3/0, 4/1)**
   **PRIEST #1 [5] [4] [3] [2] [1]**
   **PRIEST #2 [5] [4] [3] [2] [1]**

If you defeat both priests, go to section 52.

# SECTION 50
# The Fleeing Ghost

As the Hukka priests and braves approach, you gather the baubles given to you by the worshipers and walk quickly toward the forest.

When the Hukkas realize you are intent on leaving, the elders pick up stones and clods of dirt and hurl them at you. Seeing that the line of braves and priests is moving hurriedly now, you bolt into the forest.

The Hukka elders try to follow you, but your powerful legs, made more powerful by fear of what will happen to you if the braves catch up with you, drive you onward at an incredible rate.

Throughout the night, you run, dogged by the sound of Hukka drums and war cries. Slowly, the dawn comes. Scaling a tall tree, you peer down into the forest below you. No Hukkas pursue you. Somehow, you have gotten away from them.

Heading into the deep woods, you finger the baubles. Now, when you reach Suthorp, you will have something to trade. Run quickly to Section 10.

# SECTION 51
# Where Three Corridors Meet

You have to come to the intersection of three corridors. To the south, you hear loud growling sounds, to the southwest is the corridor that leads to the main entrance chamber, and to the north is a dark passage. At your feet, you see scattered remnants of Dahlia leaf heading in a trail north and southeast.

Behind you, you hear the sounds of Slith guards approaching.

Return to the map.

# SECTION 52
## Unscathed by the Hukka Priests

You stand at the top of the burial mound, the vanquished Hukka priests sprawled at your feet. The Hukka tribe drops to their knees and prays fervently. You motion to the gold trunk, and two timid braves lay it before you. Greed welling in your heart, you motion for them to open it. Instead of the jewels you hoped for, you see that the box is filled with severed heads!

A wave of nausea wells up in you, for some of the heads are Ratikkans you have known!

Seeing that there are no more jewels to be had, you pick up the baubles given to you by the Hukkas, bow ceremoniously, and walk quickly into the forest. As you walk, the Hukkas chant in reverence.

When you have walked into the forest and are out of sight, you break into a full run.

Throughout the night you run, and by dawn, your legs are sore and you stop for rest. Regain *3 hit points* and *2 experience marks*. The baubles given to you should bring 150 gold pieces in the markets at Suthorp.

Waking up in the afternoon, you head east, hoping to intersect with the Ancient Road to Suthorp.

Find your way to Section 10.

# SECTION 53
# Antoth's Grotto

You warily step into Antoth's Grotto. Holding your sword, ready to slay the man should he turn treacherous, you follow him. Suddenly, both of your arms and your feet are grabbed simultaneously. You turn to try and fight, but can only free your sword hand. Four clawed hands reach out. Antoth draws a short sword and lunges at you.

In the dim light, you see that he is not at all the decrepit old man you thought he was; rather, he is a made-up Slith Guard.

You must cut all of the hands off *and* fight Antoth. All opponents attack you during each turn. You may attack them in any order.

**SAGARD (LEVEL 3: 1/1, 2/1, 3/2, 4/3)**
[20] [19] [18] [17] [16] [15] [14] [13] [12] [11] [10]
[9] [8] [7] [6] [5] [4] [3] [2] [1] **(Begin the book again.)**

**ANTOTH (LEVEL 2: 1/0, 2/1, 3/1, 4/2)**
[10] [9] [8] [7] [6] [5] [4] [3] [2] [1]

**CLAWED HANDS (LEVEL 3: 1/1, 2/1, 3/2, 4/3)**
    **HAND #1** [4] [3] [2] [1]
    **HAND #2** [4] [3] [2] [1]
    **HAND #3** [4] [3] [2] [1]
    **HAND #4** [4] [3] [2] [1]

When you have defeated all of them, proceed on with the map. It is not considered crossing your line to leave Antoth's lair.

# SECTION 54
# Intruders in the Hukka Tomb

Blackness overtakes you as you fall into the Hukka tomb. For minutes, your mind swirls in a vast array of violent images. Slowly, you recover consciousness and discover that you are not in a tomb at all, but are in a secret room.

You recognize that the Hukkas are fighting Sliths. Crawling to shadows, you also realize that in all of the confusion, you have been forgotten. In the flickering torchlight of combat, it begins to dawn on you exactly what is taking place. The Sliths have built a secret room underneath a Hukka burial mound, and as evidenced by several costumes and jars of makeup like those used by traveling actors, they have been impersonating the dead Hukka hero for the purposes of demanding jeweled offerings.

Your entry into the scene disrupted their sinister plans, and now the Hukkas, realizing they have been deceived, exact a bloody revenge.

You are about to encounter the first battle of the Sagard Series. In this battle, 20 Hukkas fight 9 Sliths.

You want to see both sides annihilate each other,

because once one side is decimated, you will have to fight all of the survivors.

*Combat works like this:* Sliths attack first. Flip the pages for each Slith. Each time you flip a 3 or a 4, cross 1 Hukka off the page. Then, flip for all of the surviving Hukkas, and each time you flip a 4, cross off a Slith. Then, count up the number of surviving Sliths and repeat the process until one side is wiped out.

Sagard's role in the battle is as follows: Before each combat, Sagard may want to even up the odds by attacking either the Hukkas or the Sliths. Sagard always gets the first swing. All Hukkas are Level 1 fighters with 10 hit points. All Sliths are Level 2 fighters with 15 hit points.

The following tables are to be used for all such attacks. If you need more, you can reuse ones you have already used.

You may *not* flee this battle.

If Sagard dies, begin the book again.

If all of the others are dead, go to Section 55.

**SAGARD (LEVEL 3: 1/1, 2/1, 3/2, 4/3)**
[20] [19] [18] [17] [16] [15] [14] [13] [12] [11] [10] [9] [8] [7] [6] [5] [4] [3] [2] [1] (**Begin the book again.**)

*(continued on next page)*

**HUKKAS (LEVEL 1: 1/0, 2/0, 3/1, 4/1)**
    **HUKKA #1** [10] [9] [8] [7] [6] [5] [4] [3] [2] [1]
    **HUKKA #2** [10] [9] [8] [7] [6] [5] [4] [3] [2] [1]
    **HUKKA #3** [10] [9] [8] [7] [6] [5] [4] [3] [2] [1]
    **HUKKA #4** [10] [9] [8] [7] [6] [5] [4] [3] [2] [1]
    **HUKKA #5** [10] [9] [8] [7] [6] [5] [4] [3] [2] [1]

**SLITHS (LEVEL 2: 1/0, 2/1, 3/1, 4/2)**
    **SLITH #1** [15] [14] [13] [12] [11] [10] [9] [8] [7] [6] [5] [4] [3] [2] [1]
    **SLITH #2** [15] [14] [13] [12] [11] [10] [9] [8] [7] [6] [5] [4] [3] [2] [1]
    **SLITH #3** [15] [14] [13] [12] [11] [10] [9] [8] [7] [6] [5] [4] [3] [2] [1]
    **SLITH #4** [15] [14] [13] [12] [11] [10] [9] [8] [7] [6] [5] [4] [3] [2] [1]

# SECTION 55
# After the Battle

Hukkas and Sliths litter the tomb. With your last remaining strength, you climb out of the tomb.

Dawn has broken. Hukka wives and elders are sobbing. Nobody raises a hand to stop you, for though you might be the enemy, you have also proved yourself to be a brave warrior. As you leave, you stoop to pick up the baubles of the Hukkas.

Once you are safely out of the reach of any Hukkas, you view the baubles and eat the food. The baubles will be worth 150 gold pieces in the city and the food brings back your strength. Gain *10 hit points* and *2 experience marks* plus *1 mark* for each opponent you defeated.

Victorious, head to Section 10.

# SECTION 56
# The Slith Maiden

You hear moans through a doorway to the south. Looking inside, you see a gruesome scene. A beautiful Slith woman is chained to a stone table. Her eyes look to you mournfully, pleadingly. She shouts something to you in a language you don't understand. Your nose is struck by the smell of tainted flesh, and from the chamber you hear a loud growling sound. You can try to save her in Section 58.

Or, turning a deaf ear, you can head west, where you see only the outer light of the main hallway, or head east around a corner. Dahlia leaf is scattered on the floor in both directions.

Draw your line and advance to the next Section.

# SECTION 57
# The Hukka Ghost

Slowly, you climb the sheer side of the hole, your feet slipping on the moist dirt. Nearing the top, you hear a droning Hukka incantation to the dead.

Hoping to surprise them, you jump catlike out of

the hole, screaming a war cry and waving your sword.

Before you deliver a death-dealing blow, you discover that the Hukkas before you are not warriors, but old men, young women, and children. Instead of jumping to arms, they bow to you, praying feverishly. Dismayed for a moment, you realize that they believe you are the incarnation of the interred Hukka. Sheathing your sword, you raise your arms, imitating a Hukka ghost.

After a few moments of fervent chanting they bring food, and you eat. Regain 7 *hit points*. As you eat, they bring you beautiful objects—beads, small talismen, and other trinkets worth at least 150 gold pieces.

As the morning star glows on the horizon, and the Hukka women dance, you see a long procession of torches drifting toward you from the hills. You do not know who carries the torches. Do you want to find out?

You are of two minds. Do you rise like the "spirit" that you are and jaunt into the woods (go to Section 60) with the baubles they have given you? Or do you wait for the line of torch bearers to arrive, so you can try for more treasure later (Go to Section 49)?

# SECTION 58
# The Sacrifice Chamber

You run to the woman on the table with your sword drawn. Suddenly, out of the corner of your eye, you see a long, hairy arm reach out for you.

Flip: If you get an even number, go to Section 48; if you get an odd number, keep reading.

The monster's arm misses you. Turning, you see that a gigantic, hairy creature—a hideous cross between a bear and a reptile—is chained to the wall in the next room. It slashes its hideous claws toward you as you raise your sword to free the chained woman.

With two deft swipes of your blade, you have shattered her chains. Suddenly, the woman's form metamorphoses. Her beautiful face turns green and demonic, wings sprout from her shoulders, long, daggerlike nails spring from her fingers and her feet turn to hideous claws. Far from an innocent Slith woman, she is a demon placed in the chamber to lure adventurers to a screaming doom.

You should have recalled the warning of the map: "Trust nobody in the Tomb of the Green Hydra." You must fight the demon.

**SAGARD (LEVEL 3: 1/1, 2/1, 3/2, 4/3)**
[20] [19] [18] [17] [16] [15] [14] [13] [12] [11] [10]
[9] [8] [7] [6] [5] [4] [3] [2] [1] **(Begin the book
again.)**

**SHE-DEMON (LEVEL 4: 1/1, 2/2, 3/3, 4/3)**
[10] [9] [8] [7] [6] [5] [4] [3] [2] [1] **(She is defeated.
Gain 2 *experience marks*. You are at Section P.
Return to map and draw a line to your next destination.)**

# SECTION 59
# The Black Pit

You have come upon a deep pit. Looking down,
you hear the sound of running water. Behind you,
you hear the clumsy sounds of Slith Guards. You
may do one of two things. You may either try to
jump across the pit, or you may turn around. If you
turn around, go to Section 75.

You may either succeed or fail to cross the pit.
Flip the pages. Even, go to Section 86; odd, draw a
line across the pit and continue onward.

# SECTION 60
# While the Getting Is Good

As the procession grows closer you see that it is composed of Hukka braves and priests. Knowing that a brutal fate awaits you if you are discovered, you slowly rise and gather the baubles given you by the worshipers and, in your most spiritual manner, step to the forest. As you recede into the woods, they chant.

As they realize you are leaving, their mood changes. The elders pick up stones and clods of dirt and hurl them at you. Dropping all pretense, you bolt into the forest, following the Southern Star.

The Hukka elders try to follow you, but your steel-hewed legs carry you far away.

Throughout the night, you run. Slowly, the dawn comes. Scaling a tall tree, you peer down into the forest below you. No Hukkas pursue you. Somehow, you have gotten away from them.

Heading into the deep woods, you finger the baubles. Now, when you reach Suthorp, you will have something to trade.

Run quickly to Section 10.

# SECTION 61
## The Dark Intersection

You stand at the intersection of several corridors. To your southwest is a black drop pit. You might be able to escape through it. Pick a corridor and keep going.

# SECTION 62
## The Too-Safe Hall

As you traverse the long hallway, you are jumped by two Slith Guards. They attack first. You must flip a 4 to flee.

**SAGARD (LEVEL 4: 1/1, 2/2, 3/3, 4/3)**
[25] [24] [23] [22] [21] [20] [19] [18] [17] [16] [15] [14] [13] [12] [11] [10] [9] [8] [7] [6] [5] [4] [3] [2] [1] (Begin the book again.)

**SLITH GUARDS (LEVEL 3: 1/1, 2/1, 3/2, 4/3)**
  GUARD #1 [15] [14] [13] [12] [11] [10] [9] [8] [7] [6] [5] [4] [3] [2] [1]
  GUARD #2 [15] [14] [13] [12] [11] [10] [9] [8] [7] [6] [5] [4] [3] [2] [1]

When you have defeated your opponents, Gain 2 *experience marks* and return to the map.

If you successfully flee, return to the map.

# SECTION 63
# The Lighted Hallway

A thick taper sends oily black smoke through the tomb. In its flickering light, which makes the wall jump with ominous shadows, you see a pile of burned rubble on the floor.

Sifting through the rubble with your sword, you hit upon a charred skull and a burned jewel and can only come to one conclusion: Through some demonic means, a man was burned alive on this spot!

Not far away from you is a corridor; looking past it, you spot a stairway that might be some kind of an escape route from the tomb.

If you want to take it, go to Section 2. Otherwise, keep going.

# SECTION 64
# The Corridor

As you dash through the corridor, you hear a loud *psst* sound, as if somebody is calling you. Spinning around, you see the pale face of a man close to death peering out at you.

"Ratikkan!" he urgently whispers to you. "Come this way!"

"Identify yourself before I cut you down!" you demand.

"I am Antoth, a builder. Weeks ago, the architect escaped and left me for dead. I have been hiding here ever since."

"And what good are you to me?" you ask.

"I know all of the secrets of the tomb. If you will take me with you, I will be your guide."

Just then, you hear the footsteps of Slith Guards. Antoth motions for you to join him in his hiding place.

You have to make a quick decision. If you join him, go to Section 53. If not, proceed with the map.

# SECTION 65
# Cut by the Priests

Blood trickles from your arm. The Hukka crowd lets out a gasp of surprise. Ghosts don't bleed. Suddenly your problems with the priests are minimal. The whole tribe rushes you.

Raising your sword, you prepare for a final, bloody battle, but the sheer weight of the charging throng knocks you backward into the pit.

Your mind blurs with thoughts of your hideous death as you plummet through the darkness. You think of being pelted with their arrows and of being buried alive, but as you hit the bottom of the pit, you hear a dull wooden thud and a cracking sound.

Before you can scramble to your feet, a pair of Hukka braves land next to you, smashing the timbers which support the floor of the mound, and all three of you crash into a chamber below.

Fall quickly to Section 54.

# SECTION 66
## Guards

Two black-leather-clad Slith Guards carrying battle-axes protect the entrance to the Chamber. As you are still disguised as a Dahlia carrier, they let you pass.

However, if you take anything unordained from the tomb, they will attack you.

Proceed to Section 67.

# SECTION 67
## The Arrow Chamber

The sickly smoke of a burning taper clouds the chamber. In the center of the triangular vault is a garish green statue a foot high with an enormous green jewel embedded in the forehead. Looking over your shoulder, you see that you are being watched by the guards. In one corner of the room are six arrows. There are twenty jewels on the floor, placed there as if in offering to the statue. You contemplate looting the tomb, but know you might have to fight the guards as a consequence.

Write down all of the things you take and proceed to Section 68.

# SECTION 68
# Leaving the Arrow Chamber

If you took only the arrows, you can proceed farther on the map. However, if you took anything else, the Slith Guards attack you.

SAGARD (LEVEL 3: 1/1, 2/1, 3/2, 4/3)
[20] [19] [18] [17] [16] [15] [14] [13] [12] [11] [10] [9] [8] [7] [6] [5] [4] [3] [2] [1] (Begin the book again.)

SLITH GUARDS (LEVEL 3: 1/1, 2/1, 3/2, 4/3)
   GUARD #1 [15] [14] [13] [12] [11] [10] [9] [8] [7] [6] [5] [4] [3] [2] [1]
   GUARD #2 [15] [14] [13] [12] [11] [10] [9] [8] [7] [6] [5] [4] [3] [2] [1]

When you defeat both guards, take whatever you want from the tomb.

If you successfully flee, drop all booty and keep moving.

# SECTION 69
# The Corridor

You stand in a dank corridor. A spilled trail of Night Dahlia leads southward and then turns right, while directly to the west is a dark hole which you can jump into to try to get out of the tomb.

Suddenly, in the darkness, you come upon a group of Dahlia carriers. In their hands are buckets of brown fluid. From the thick smell that seems to come from it, you guess that it is Dahlia Oil. If you want to dip the arrows into it, you can. Note it on your *status chart*.

The Dahlia carriers peer at you with drained, empty eyes as you step past them.

"Carry my burden for me," one of them calls, staggering toward you.

You dodge him as he reaches out to grab you, but his clawed hands rip your garb, making your sword and Ratikkan clothing plainly visible.

Proceed farther, if you dare.

# SECTION 70
# The Oil Chamber

You cautiously step to the chamber expecting to find guards at the entrance. Much to your surprise, you discover the guards crumpled on the floor, with daggers sticking in their backs. Stepping over them, you enter the chamber cautiously, for whoever murdered the guards may still be in there.

The air inside the chamber is thick from Dahlia smoke which rises from a bubbling caldron in the center of the room.

Near the caldron is a pile of *golden bars*, stacked in a precariously balanced inverted pyramid shape. You could carry perhaps five of them.

Not far from the bars, you spy a wooden chest. Its lock is so frail that a single swing with your sword could break it open.

If you take any of these things, or dip anything into the Dahlia Oil, note this on your *status chart* and go to Section 76.

# SECTION 71
# Hiding from the Hukkas

The Hukka chant drones on for hours as you hide in the deep hole, and then suddenly it dies. Thinking the ceremony is over, you let out a sigh of relief, but suddenly, you are bathed in firelight.

Looking up in horror, you see two priests holding flickering torches. Before you can react, they bellow outraged cries.

Suddenly two Hukka braves jump down after you . . .

Raising your sword, you expect a furious battle, but as they hit the bottom of the hole, you hear the loud crack of wood breaking, and you tumble into the darkness of the ancient tomb.

Fall blindly to Section 54.

# SECTION 72
# A Noise in the Crypt

With one crack of your sword, you break the lock. Before you can fling open the chest, the Slith Guards, who appeared to be dead, charge through the doorway. You realize that they were playing possum. The fake daggers that were sticking to them were props.

You must fight the guards for one round before fleeing. If you flee, lose everything you have taken from the tomb, save for the bow and arrows. Continue on the map.

SAGARD (LEVEL 3: 1/1, 2/1, 3/2, 4/3)
[20] [19] [18] [17] [16] [15] [14] [13] [12] [11] [10]
[9] [8] [7] [6] [5] [4] [3] [2] [1] (Begin the book again.)

(continued on next page)

**SLITH GUARDS (LEVEL 3: 1/1, 2/1, 3/2, 4/3)**
  **GUARD #1** [15] [14] [13] [12] [11] [10] [9] [8]
[7] [6] [5] [4] [3] [2] [1]
  **GUARD #2** [15] [14] [13] [12] [11] [10] [9] [8]
[7] [6] [5] [4] [3] [2] [1]

When you have defeated both guards (gain *3 experience marks*), you have the option of either opening the chest or continuing on the map.

If you open the chest, go to Section 74.

# SECTION 73
# The Jewel and Advice

"I will trust you," you say to the priest.

You take the jewel from his icy hand and he points around the corner. "Around two corners, you shall find a dark pit. Jump into the pit and you shall find safety."

"You lie!" you say, noticing that the jewel seems slightly warm in your hand.

"I speak the truth," he responds.

Before you can draw your sword the jewel becomes a burning coal in your hand. Instinctively, you try to drop the jewel, but it is stuck to your hand. The priests flee down the hall as you scream in agony, vainly trying to remove the jewel from your burning hand.

The flames spread up your arm and approach your head. You have been tricked. You should have remembered to trust nobody in the Tomb of the Green Hydra.

As the fire engulfs your body, you realize that you will soon be a burned pile of ashes littering the chamber.

Begin this book again.

# SECTION 74
# Opening the Chest

You fling the chest open and suddenly a lick of flame shoots out at you giving you *3 points of damage.* Jumping back, you see that you have let out ten flamebats, normally used to keep the caldron lit.

The flamebats shoot out of the chest and whirl around you, spitting flame at you as you wheel around fighting them. By arcing your sword around in the air, you can probably hit one, killing one flamebat for each point of damage your sword does. Thus, if you flip a 4, you will kill three flamebats (plus another, if you have the Valkyrie Sword).

Flamebats do one point of damage each time you flip a 4 no matter what kind of armor you are wearing. All flamebats are Level 1 fighters.

SAGARD'S (LEVEL 3: 1/1, 2/1, 3/2, 4/3)
[20] [19] [18] [17] [16] [15] [14] [13] [12] [11] [10]
[9] [8] [7] [6] [5] [4] [3] [2] [1] (Begin the book again.)

When you have defeated all of the flamebats, gain *2 experience marks*, take your booty, and continue on the map.

# SECTION 75
# Crossing Your Path

Suddenly, you make out two Slith Guards. These are not the normal Slith Fighters. Instead, they are clad in black mail and wear conical helmets. They are Elite Slith Guards who stand in front of you, their long, thin swords drawn, their hellish eyes glowing and broken teeth smiling.

Trying to avoid them, you turn to run, but to no avail. Two more Slith Guards stand behind you. Trapped in the corridor, you have no hope for escape. You must fight the four Slith Guards.

Drawing your blade, you swing first.

**SAGARD (LEVEL 3: 1/1, 2/1, 3/2, 4/3)**
[20] [19] [18] [17] [16] [15] [14] [13] [12] [11] [10] [9] [8] [7] [6] [5] [4] [3] [2] [1] (Begin the book again.)

**ELITE SLITH GUARD #1 (LEVEL 4: 1/1, 2/2, 3/3, 4/3)**
[15] [14] [13] [12] [11] [10] [9] [8] [7] [6] [5] [4] [3] [2] [1]

**ELITE SLITH GUARD #2 (LEVEL 3: 1/1, 2/1, 3/2, 4/3)**
[17] [16] [15] [14] [13] [12] [11] [10] [9] [8] [7] [6] [5] [4] [3] [2] [1]

(continued on next page)

**ELITE SLITH GUARD #3 (LEVEL 2: 1/0, 2/1, 3/1, 4/2)**
[20] [19] [18] [17] [16] [15] [14] [13] [12] [11] [10] [9] [8] [7] [6] [5] [4] [3] [2] [1]

**ELITE SLITH GUARD #4 (LEVEL 3: 1/1, 2/1, 3/2, 4/3)**
[17] [16] [15] [14] [13] [12] [11] [10] [9] [8] [7] [6] [5] [4] [3] [2] [1]

You may *not* flee.

If you defeat all four Slith Guards, gain 7 *experience marks* and continue your journey, free to cross your path anytime you want.

# SECTION 76
# The Oil Chamber

If you took nothing from the chamber except Dahlia Oil, keep moving on the map. If you tried to break into the chest, flip the pages: If you get an even number, go to Section 72; if you get an odd number, go to Section 74. If you left the chest alone, but wanted the gold, keep reading.

If you tried to take the gold bars, flip the pages: If you get an even number, return to the map and keep moving; if you get an odd number, go to Section 80. If you did not try to take the gold bars, keep moving.

# 4

# SECTION 77
# The Hydra Chamber

Entering the Hydra Chamber, you are over-whelmed by the unholy stench of reptile and burned Night Dahlia—sickly sweet death.

At the far side of the chamber sleeps a beast hideous beyond description. Seven heads, half-reptile and half-human, protrude on long necks from a grotesque reptilian body. As you step closer to the revolting sight, one eye opens.

At this point, you may fire any missile weapons you have. If you fire arrows dipped in Dahlia Oil, flip for each of the seven arrows you have. If you flip an even number, the head is knocked out of combat (cross it off the combat chart on the next page). If you flip an odd number, the arrow misses. If you are throwing any other weapon, use the in-structions you were given when you gained that weapon.

Mark your hits on the Hydra combat chart.

After you fire your projectiles, the Hydra sud-denly comes to life. Its eyes, flaming with hatred, glare at you. For a moment it appears that the Hy-dra is restrained by its chain, but one of the heads turns and spits acid on the chain. Smoke rises, and in seconds, the chain melts to the floor in a bub-bling puddle of molten metal. Then the horrific beast slithers toward you.

To turn your back on the Hydra would mean instant death; thus, you must fight it to the death. You strike first, but each of the Hydra's remaining heads fights every turn.

**SAGARD (LEVEL 3: 1/1, 2/1, 3/2, 4/3)**
[20] [19] [18] [17] [16] [15] [14] [13] [12] [11] [10] [9] [8] [7] [6] [5] [4] [3] [2] [1] (Begin the book again.)

**HYDRA'S HEADS (LEVEL 5: 1/2, 2/3, 3/3, 4/4)**
   **HEAD #1** [10] [9] [8] [7] [6] [5] [4] [3] [2] [1]
   **HEAD #2** [10] [9] [8] [7] [6] [5] [4] [3] [2] [1]
   **HEAD #3** [10] [9] [8] [7] [6] [5] [4] [3] [2] [1]
   **HEAD #4** [10] [9] [8] [7] [6] [5] [4] [3] [2] [1]
   **HEAD #5** [10] [9] [8] [7] [6] [5] [4] [3] [2] [1]
   **HEAD #6** [10] [9] [8] [7] [6] [5] [4] [3] [2] [1]
   **HEAD #7** [10] [9] [8] [7] [6] [5] [4] [3] [2] [1]

If you defeat the Hydra, gain *10 experience marks* and return to the map.

# SECTION 78
# The Long Hallway

Racing down the long, dark hallway, you pull a torch from the wall and throw it behind you. It tumbles through the air, hits the floor, and shatters, spilling lamp oil. The lamp oil bursts into flames, thus cutting off any pursuing guards but also eliminating your chances of crossing that hallway again.

Continuing up the corridor, you spy four human shapes just yards away. Gripping your sword tightly in your hand, you charge them.

Drawing closer, you realize that they are Slith Priests. Instead of turning to fight, they stare at you with sad eyes—looking as if they are severely under the influence of Night Dahlia.

One of them, a particularly ancient-looking man, turns to you. "You know not what you do, Ratik-kan."

The others listlessly nod in agreement.

"Should you kill the Hydra, you will unleash a terror that would consume the entire Isle of Slith."

"The Sliths did not worry much about spreading their evil through Ratik."

"Spare yourself and spare us, Ratikkan. Turn away. I will show you an escape route and give you this jewel."

The priest holds out a ruby of immense size which seems to let out its own light in the tomb.

At this point, you may do one of three things. You may take the jewel and the priest's advice (go to Section 73), you may take the jewel and forget the advice (go to Section 79), or you may slide past the Sliths and continue your journey (go back to the map).

# SECTION 79
# Taking the Jewel

"I have no need of your advice, old man, but I will take the jewel." With that, you pull the glowing ruby from his icy hand and fling him aside. None of the others lift a weapon to stop you as you step around the corner.

Slowly, as you step down the gloomy corridors, toward the Hydra Chamber, you realize that the jewel is burning hot. Instinctively, you try to drop the jewel, but it is stuck to your hand. In the distance, you hear the cackling laughter of the priests.

Your hand is in flames. Your agonized screams

echo through the tomb. There is no way to put out the flaming agony.

The flames spread up your arm to your head. You have been tricked. You should have remembered to trust nobody in the Tomb of the Green Hydra.

As the fire engulfs your body, you realize that you will soon be a charred heap of blackened rubble.

Begin this book again.

# SECTION 80
# The Gold Bars

As you try to take the gold bars, a whiff of Dahlia Oil overtakes you and you clumsily tip the gold pyramid. The entire stack of gold collapses, and a loud clang echoes throughout the chamber.

Suddenly the guards who appeared to be dead charge through the doorway. You realize that they were playing possum. The fake daggers that were sticking to them were props.

You must fight the guards for one round before fleeing. If you flee, you lose everything from the tomb but your weapons, then continue on the map.

**SAGARD (LEVEL 3: 1/1, 2/1, 3/2, 4/3)**
[20] [19] [18] [17] [16] [15] [14] [13] [12] [11] [10] [9] [8] [7] [6] [5] [4] [3] [2] [1] (**Begin the book again.**)

**SLITH GUARDS (LEVEL 3: 1/1, 2/1, 3/2, 4/3)**
   **GUARD #1** [15] [14] [13] [12] [11] [10] [9] [8] [7] [6] [5] [4] [3] [2] [1]
   **GUARD #2** [15] [14] [13] [12] [11] [10] [9] [8] [7] [6] [5] [4] [3] [2] [1]

When you have defeated both guards, mark the *gold bars* on your *status chart*, gain *3 experience marks*, and continue on the map.

# SECTION 81
# Defeating the Murderous Shipmates

Swarny Pate eyes his two shipmates, who lie face down on the deck, and drops his cutlass. Gain 2 *experience marks*.

"Kill me and you'll never find your way to the island," he says.

"Cross me and you will find yourself in the belly of a shark," you respond.

He shrugs and steps to the rudder. "Fair enough . . ."

As he sails, you dump the bodies of the two shipmates into the dark, velvety sea. They float for just a moment, and then two triangular fins emerge from the depths and the two bodies vanish in a bubbling frenzy.

Eating the food that his murderous shipmates will no longer need, you regain 5 *hit points*.

Swarny Pate points, and you gain your first view of the Isle of Slith. A broken volcanic cone thrusts bizarrely from the azure sea. As you draw closer, you see that the lava octopus sends gnarled tentacles of flowing molten rock into the bubbling sea, surrounding the island with a thick, steamy mist.

Approaching the island, you see that even beneath the water there are molten gashes on the coastal floor.

Your small craft gets very hot as it draws closer to shore, and you are startled to see Swarny drop a small bird into the water which emerges completely boiled a few moments later.

As you sail to the far side of the Isle, you realize that this is perhaps the most inhospitable place on the planet. Volcanic gas rises from molten gashes in the treeless terrain, and fresh eruptions shake the air like a thunderstorm.

The far side of the island is slightly more hospitable. You see living trees and, here and there, catch sight of a black-sailed Slith ship wending its way through the mists and shiny, jagged rocks that surround the island.

By late afternoon, Swarny Pate lands the boat in a small, relatively hospitable inlet.

Go to Section 90.

# SECTION 82
## Escape Stairs

Your heart pounds as you charge down the stairs, which seem to descend to the center of the earth. Behind you, you hear the shouts of Slith Guards.

Reaching the bottom of the stairs, you find yourself on a long, narrow ridge in an underground cavern. Far below, a river of molten lava flows, and high above you is a forest of hanging stalactites. At the far end of the cavern, nearly a mile away, a thin shaft of light cuts through the malevolent gloom.

Behind you, Slith Guards run down the stairs, shouting. Taking flight across the narrow ridge, you try not to look down as arrows whiz past your ears. Flip the pages four times and take 1 point of damage for each 1 you flip. If that kills you—well, you have made a valiant attempt.

Reaching the shaft of light, you stand at the mouth of a cave. Below you, the lava river pours into the boiling ocean. Arrows shower down on you, and it looks as if there is no escape. Flip the pages four more times and take 1 hit point for each even number you flip.

With perfect timing, a red-masted ship sails around a jutting rock in the boiling ocean. Looking more closely, you see that its hull is made of finely chiseled stone, and it is piloted by a dashing fellow. Standing next to him is none other than Ketza Kota. She waves to you as the boat draws nearer. Arrows rain down on the boat but, miraculously, none of them hit the passengers.

As the boat draws close to you, you jump onto it. Ketza Kota wraps her arms around you, and a gust of wind pulls your boat out of the bay and to the open ocean. Gain *1 experience mark.*

Looking back, you see the Isle of Slith in turmoil. Twenty-foot-tall Fire Demons smash their way out of the tomb and ravage the Isle. Panicking Sliths, carrying large bails of Night Dahlia, scramble for their ships. Some make it, while others are crushed by enormous volcanic rocks thrown by the monsters.

By nightfall, you reach shore on the Pirate Isle, St. Koal, with Ketza Kota. Together, you watch the blood-red sun sink over the ocean.

As dusk settles in, you see a burst of red on the horizon, and know that the Isle of Slith and the evil that radiated from it have been destroyed. Ketza Kota looks sad for a moment, and then smiles. "If we have gained nothing, we have at least gained each other."

If you have booty, you may take it to the trading shop in Section 88.

# SECTION 83
# The Hall of Bones

Following the trail of bones in the corridor, you enter a room filled with the stench of death. Skeletons are piled nearly to the ceiling. Mingled with the bones are broken swords, crushed maces and scraps of tattered clothing.

Hearing footsteps, you conceal yourself among the corpses, and a pair of Slith Guards blindly step past. If you want to rummage through the bones in search of anything, continue reading. If not, return to the map.

Thrashing through the bones yields you *20 Slith coins* (mark them on your *status chart*) and little else, other than a few bits of broken weapons. Finally, however, you come upon a black-robed skeleton still covered with leathery flesh. On its face is a twisted smile, and his withering hands seem to point to *7 fire darts* in his sash.

Carefully, you remove the sash and wrap it around your waist. You can throw two darts during any round of combat. When you throw them, flip the pages. If you flip anything but a 4, they will knock out anything they hit. These are powerful *weapons;* use them sparingly.

Note these on the *status chart* and move onward.

# SECTION 84
## Escape Pit

Having left a large corridor, you turn down a smaller one. It leads to a dark void. You stand before a neatly chiseled hole outlined with Slith hieroglyphics. If you had more time, you might be able to read them, but you hear the sound of Slith Guards behind you. You may either turn and fight the guards (go to Section 85), or you may jump into the pit. If you jump into the pit, flip the pages. If the number is even, go to Section 86; if the number is odd, go to Section 89.

# SECTION 85
## Fighting the Slith Guards

Standing at the edge of the escape pit, you turn and see two Slith Guards in chain mail approaching. Flip to see who attacks first. If you flip a 1 or 2, you attack first; if you flip a 3 or 4, they attack first.

SAGARD (LEVEL 3: 1/1, 2/1, 3/2, 4/3)
[20] [19] [18] [17] [16] [15] [14] [13] [12] [11] [10]
[9] [8] [7] [6] [5] [4] [3] [2] [1] (Begin the book again.)

(continued on next page)

**SLITH GUARDS (LEVEL 3: 1/1, 2/1, 3/2, 4/3)**
    **GUARD #1** [17] [16] [15] [14] [13] [12] [11] [10] [9] [8] [7] [6] [5] [4] [3] [2] [1]
    **GUARD #2** [17] [16] [15] [14] [13] [12] [11] [10] [9] [8] [7] [6] [5] [4] [3] [2] [1]

If you defeat both Slith Guards, gain *4 experience marks* and continue on your path, ignoring the rule about crossing your path until you are out of the corridor that led to the drop pit.

If you don't have any *chain mail*, you may take it off one of the guards. When wearing it, deduct 1 damage point from every attack against you.

You may *not* flee; however, you may jump. If you do, flip the pages. If you get an even number, go to Section 86; if you get an odd number, go to Section 89.


# SECTION 86
# The Drop Pit

You jump into the pit. Below you is blackness. You plummet through the darkness until you see a reddish glow far below you. In your last moments alive, you realize that you have just jumped into a lava river. Begin the book again.

# SECTION 87
# Defeating the Muckmonga

Dangerously close to death, the Muckmonga dives into the pool of muck (gain 3 *experience marks*). You turn and make your way through the stinking filth as quickly as you can, leaving him far behind.

Following the tunnel to the end, you step out onto a lava beach, covered in oozing slime.

For days you sit on the beach, tired, filthy, and hungry, wondering how you are going to get away. Just as you think about turning yourself in to the Sliths and volunteering in their army, another adventurer stumbles out of the caves, covered in filth.

He laughs when he sees your condition, and happily shows his treasure. He holds a small statue of a hydra, several coins and a large green jewel.

You have some similar treasure and are puzzled about how this came to be, but rather than raise his suspicion or ire, you ask him if he has a boat. Indeed he does, and he will sail you off this island for half of your treasure. As you have little choice in the matter, you go along with him.

Together you make your way to his boat and spend several days weaving through an unbelievable array of islands, nearly being squashed under the hulls of several ships on the way.

Finally you land on a large island where a number of old salts guffaw loudly when they see your disheveled condition, and follow you into a trading shop. To see what your treasures are worth, go to Section 88.

# SECTION 88
# The Trading Shop

You show the treasures you gained from the Tomb of the Green Hydra to an old salt who is just about as jaded as they come. To see what you got for each one, go down the list.

SLITH COINS: These are collector's items. Gain *100 gold pieces.*

HYDRA STATUE: The trader laughs and points to a shelf filled with identical statues. It seems that the Sliths put this one into their tomb to trip you up. It is worth nothing except as a souvenir.

SLITH JEWELS: Like the statue, these are phonies designed to fool adventurers and give them an incentive to get out of the tomb thinking they have made a fortune.

THE HYDRA'S MANACLE: This is the most valuable item you have. Gain *1,000 gold pieces* for it, completely unaware that you have been hosed. A true collector would pay ten times that amount.

GOLD BARS: Like everything else deliberately put in the tombs to fool adventurers, these are only plated. Melted down, they add up to *1 gold piece*.

Note your treasure and all of your weapons and armor on the *status chart*, for everything will come in handy in the next book.

# SECTION 89
# The Drop Pit

You fall for several moments in darkness. Whizzing through the night, you prepare for death, but much to your chagrin, you land in a small, muddy pond.

There is a hideous stench in the pond, which is dimly lit by a glowing moss on the wall. Standing up, you hear a slobbering growl. In the dim, greenish light, you make out the silhouette of a grotesque creature. It is nearly ten feet tall, and looks like it is made of slightly melting wax.

"Give me your treasure and I shall let you live," it says in a burbling, inhuman voice that sounds as if it has a throat full of sludge.

Knee deep in filth, you draw your sword and stare at the creature. It is truly massive, but looks stupid and slow. It is a Muckmonga. You may either fight it to the end or, at any time, turn over all of your treasure.

**SAGARD (LEVEL 3: 1/1, 2/1, 3/2, 4/3)**
[20] [19] [18] [17] [16] [15] [14] [13] [12] [11] [10]
[9] [8] [7] [6] [5] [4] [3] [2] [1] (**Begin the book again.**)

**MUCKMONGA (LEVEL 4: 1/1, 2/2, 3/3, 4/3)**
[19] [18] [17] [16] [15] [14] [13] [12] [11] [10] [9] [8]
[7] [6] [5] [4] [3] [2] [1]

When you defeat the Muckmonga, go to Section 87.

If you turn over your treasure, go to Section 100.

# SECTION 90
# Entering the Tomb

"Fifty gold pieces now, and I'll wait for you." Swarny Pate says, his gnarled face lit by the reddish glow of the island.

You consider the offer. Swarny Pate is as treacherous as they come. However, he is your only hope of a ride off the island. If you want to take your chances on him, deduct *50 gold pieces* (if you have them) from your *status chart*.

Stepping onto the island, you are choked by a cloud of sulfurous smoke. The landscape you see is one that could only be forged in a nightmare. The ground in most places is glassy rock, save for small islands of dirt and vegetation between rivers of lava flows.

Turning around, you see Swarny Pate's boat disappear into the fog. He lets out a loud laugh and calls, "May Gak help you, Ratikkan." The boat is gone in the mist.

Trekking up the vertical lava staircase, you come in sight of the Slith village. A semicircular plot of green with white dahlia fields surrounds short walls of black, glassy stone. To the back of the city, you see what must be the tomb, a great structure of black glass with a single rectangular portal, guarded by scimitar-toting Sliths.

Climbing up the steaming island to the village, you catch sight of several people wandering as if in a stupor. Passing near them, they seem not to notice you, for their haunted eyes are glassed over and their mouths are muttering stupidly. It is not hard to guess that they are victims of the Night Dahlia.

From a low vantage point, you observe the tomb. A nearly endless procession of gray-hooded Night Dahlia carriers drifts past the guards in and out of the portal, and you resolve to gain a similar robe.

As you progress up the hill, you come upon a great open pit filled with dead Sliths—some of whom still wear their gowns. Stripping a gown from a skeleton, you don it, and rubbing ashes on your face, gain the diseased look of the Sliths.

A trail of glazed-eyed Slith Dahlia carriers marches past six Slith Guards and two enormous, gaudily painted statues of hideous monsters. You are at the rear, and though the guards eye you, they do not prevent you from entering the Tomb of the Green Hydra.

The Tomb of the Green Hydra reeks of death and evil. The corridors are narrow and cramped. The walls are of chiseled glassy rock, wet with blood and moisture. Footsteps, distant screams, and low growls echo through the structure, and you cannot help but shiver slightly at the evil that surrounds you. As you reach the first intersection, the Dahlia carriers proceed northward. Stopping in your tracks, you look back at the glowing entrance, and then to your left and right.

Go to Section 98.

# SECTION 91
## Hall of Bones

Padding down the corridor, you find yourself in deathly darkness. To the north and east you hear footsteps. Some of them are the even, marching tromp of guards, others are the soft shuffling of Dahlia carriers.

Taking refuge behind a wall, you step on something and hear a crunching sound. Looking down, you see the empty sockets and wild grin of a skull. Scanning the floor you see that it is covered with bones, which seem to be piled in a room to the west. A sign over the door reads, HALL OF BONES (in Slith hieroglyphics).

Return to the map and draw an arrow to wherever you want to go from here. You are at B.

# SECTION 92
## The Chamber of Sleep

Your path through the main artery of the tomb is cluttered with collapsed Dahlia carriers. With each step you take, an unnatural tiredness comes over you. Such is the evil effect of the Night Dahlia.

Reaching the final chamber, you find yourself in a dark room piled high with Night Dahlia. Two Slith Guards brandishing jagged swords take a slow step toward you, but their own movement is impeded by the sinister substance.

Flip the pages. If you flip an even number, go to Section 95. If you flip an odd number, go to Section 93.

# SECTION 93
## The Dahlia Guards

The Slith Guards stumble toward you. Fearing their blades, you dash out of the chamber, your mind swimming in dazed fear. The farther you get from the vile fumes of the Dahlia, the less its vile fumes affect you.

Return to the map.

# SECTION 94
# The Hydra's Guards

Rounding the corner, you encounter two guards dressed in full plate armor and carrying long glaives. Flip the pages. If you flip an even number, you have surprised them and attack first; if you flip an odd number, you have not surprised them and they attack first.

You may *not* flee them; however, you might be able to slip past them if you flip a 4 before any of your rounds of combat.

**SAGARD (LEVEL 3: 1/1, 2/1, 3/2, 4/3)**
[20] [19] [18] [17] [16] [15] [14] [13] [12] [11] [10] [9] [8] [7] [6] [5] [4] [3] [2] [1] (**Begin the book again.**)

*(continued on next page)*

**TOMB GUARDS (LEVEL 4: 1/1, 2/2, 3/3, 4/3)**

   **GUARD #1** [15] [14] [13] [12] [11] [10] [9] [8]
[7] [6] [5] [4] [3] [2] [1]

   **GUARD #2** [15] [14] [13] [12] [11] [10] [9] [8]
[7] [6] [5] [4] [3] [2] [1]

If you defeat both guards, gain *4 experience
marks* and return to the map.

If you slip past the guards, go to Section 96.


# SECTION 95
# Resisting the Night Dahlia

The two guards stumble toward you. You are
under the influence of the Night Dahlia's powerful
vapors. Before you can escape the room, the guards

swing at you, but their attacks are so weak that they are fighting at Level 2, and they are only good for five hit points. Sluggish from the Night Dahlia fumes, you fight at Level 2.

**SAGARD (LEVEL 2: 1/0, 2/1, 3/1, 4/2)**
[20] [19] [18] [17] [16] [15] [14] [13] [12] [11] [10] [9] [8] [7] [6] [5] [4] [3] [2] [1] (Begin the book again.)

**SLITH GUARDS (LEVEL 2: 1/0, 2/1, 3/1, 4/2)**
  GUARD #1 [5] [4] [3] [2] [1]
  GUARD #2 [5] [4] [3] [2] [1]

You may *not* flee.
If you defeat both guards, gain 4 *experience marks* and return to the map.

# SECTION 96
# The Third Chamber

Fleeing past the guards, you enter the third chamber.

On the far side of the triangular vault, lit by the lurid torchlight, is the most ghastly creature you have ever seen. It is an enormous reptilian beast with seven heads. Around the stout neck, from which seven serpentine necks sprout, is an enormous manacle.

This is the Green Hydra. It appears to be asleep as you enter, but when you approach it, one eye slit on one head opens.

As you ponder the hideous creature, the Slith Guards charge into the room after you. Reacting quickly, you jab your sword into the monster's scaly body.

Suddenly, all of the heads look toward you and the two Slith Guards. The guards, horrified by the hideous creature, return to their full fighting strength.

As the battle begins, you are struck by the horrifying realization that all of the Hydra's heads were once human! Where there were once teeth, there are now fangs dripping with venom; where there were once eyes, there are now only hollow slits.

For a moment, the Hydra is restrained by its chain, but one of the heads turns and spits acid on the chain. Smoke rises, and in seconds the chain drops to the floor, a bubbling puddle of molten metal.

You and the two guards must fight the Hydra to the death. If you have missile weapons, use them—instead of normal combat.

If you are using the bow and arrow, flip the pages. You hit on everything but a four. Hitting one of the heads puts it out of action for the rest of combat. Each of the Hydra's heads fights every turn. Three of them attack you and two of them attack each of the Slith Guards. If a Slith Guard dies, the head or heads attacking him will attack you. Your side strikes first.

SAGARD (LEVEL 3: 1/1, 2/1, 3/2, 4/3)
[20] [19] [18] [17] [16] [15] [14] [13] [12] [11] [10]
[9] [8] [7] [6] [5] [4] [3] [2] [1] (Begin the book again.)

**SLITH TOMB GUARDS (LEVEL 4: 1/1, 2/2, 3/3, 4/3)**

    **GUARD #1** [15] [14] [13] [12] [11] [10] [9] [8] [7] [6] [5] [4] [3] [2] [1]

    **GUARD #2** [15] [14] [13] [12] [11] [10] [9] [8] [7] [6] [5] [4] [3] [2] [1]

**HYDRA'S HEADS (LEVEL 5: 1/2, 2/3, 3/3, 4/4)**

    **HEAD #1** [10] [9] [8] [7] [6] [5] [4] [3] [2] [1]

    **HEAD #2** [10] [9] [8] [7] [6] [5] [4] [3] [2] [1]

    **HEAD #3** [10] [9] [8] [7] [6] [5] [4] [3] [2] [1]

    **HEAD #4** [10] [9] [8] [7] [6] [5] [4] [3] [2] [1]

    **HEAD #5** [10] [9] [8] [7] [6] [5] [4] [3] [2] [1]

    **HEAD #6** [10] [9] [8] [7] [6] [5] [4] [3] [2] [1]

    **HEAD #7** [10] [9] [8] [7] [6] [5] [4] [3] [2] [1]

If you kill the Hydra, gain *10 experience marks* and return to the map.

# SECTION 97
## The Wizened Priest

Apparently, Maji Mahot's congregation has dropped off a bit over the years, for the area that used to be the nave of a cathedral now houses a blacksmith shop, and while you speak to the priest, your conversation is disturbed by the loud clanging. The far end of the cathedral, which was once a chapel, is now a bakery, and your nose is tickled by the delicious scents of new cakes, thus managing to rub out the musty smell of the Priest's quarters.

"It is not often that I have visitors," the Priest begins.

You smile, embarrassed for the Priest. "Maji Mahot is highly revered in the north."

"I appreciate your sentiments, my son, but they are false. It seems that I serve an unpopular master. What have you come for?"

"I have received a coded map. I wish your advice in knowing what the words on the map mean."

You hand him the map and he takes a careful look at it. "Ah, it is a very archaic hieroglyphic map. Nothing complex here."

He points to the first line. "This line says, 'The Tomb of the Green Hydra.'"

He looks down at the map again and traces another line with his gnarled finger. "This line says, 'Trust nobody in the Tomb of the Green Hydra.'"

"Tell me about the tomb," you say.

The Priest looks up as if to answer, when suddenly you hear a rush of air and a soft thud, and you see the Priest's eyes bulge. He looks at you for a moment. "Destroy the Hydra, my son. Destroy it. Find Ketz—" Before he can finish his sentence, he collapses on the table. There is a flash of gray from the blacksmith's shop, and you see a Slith dagger sticking in the old man's back.

At this point, you probably have enough information to decode the map to be found in Section 40. If you decode it yourself, go to the section indicated in the decoded map.

If you can't decode it and want to go to the Tomb of the Green Hydra regardless of the message, go to Section 45.

To try and make contact with Ketza Kota, return to the inn (Section 42).

# SECTION 98
# Tomb Exploration

You are at the entrance to the Tomb of the Green Hydra. Draw a line to the next section you want to go to (you may not pass through a section without going to it), and go to that section in the book. After reading the section and resolving any combat that may come up, return to this map and draw a line to the section you next want to visit, and go to that page. Resolve any combat, then return to the map and trace a line to the next destination. (Make a note of this section number, as you will return to it often.)

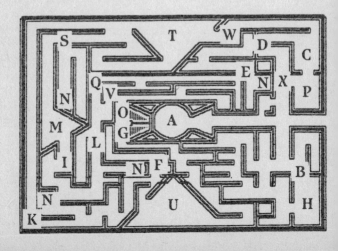

You may not return to any section twice, because it is considered to be swarming with Slith Guards. Avoid crossing your own path. If you should be forced to do so, go to Section 75.

When you reach a letter on the map, look at the list below and go to the Section indicated.

| | |
|---|---|
| A —Section 92 | M—Section 67 |
| B —Section 91 | N —Section 84 |
| C —Section 48 | O —Section  2 |
| D —Section 51 | P —Section 58 |
| E —Section 61 | Q —Section 62 |
| F —Section 94 | S —Section 69 |
| G —Section 82 | T —Section 70 |
| H —Section 83 | U —Section 77 |
| I —Section 66 | V —Section 63 |
| K —Section 78 | W—Section 59 |
| L —Section 64 | X —Section 56 |

# SECTION 99
## Treacherous Voyage

The stars glow like jewels in the death-black sky as Swarny Pate's boat sails through the murky sea. In time, when Suthorp's towers have sunk below the horizon, you make out islands silhouetted on the horizon. Most are composed of jutting rock and are probably uninhabited, but on some of them orange embers of dying fires glow.

In time, the soft rocking of the ship, the warm winds from the south, and the tranquil salt air make you drowsy. However, you know that falling asleep would be a sure invitation to be attacked by Swarny Pate and his two sinister Fexian shipmates.

Slowly, you slump over in your seat, feeling more tired than ever. Struggling to keep awake, you slit your finger on your gleaming blade. The sting keeps you awake through what might have been a night of treachery.

Before dawn you see an orange glow on the eastern horizon. "Thar she is . . ." Swarny Pate informs you. "As hellish a place as Gak has yet created."

He points, and you gain your first view of the Isle

of Slith. A broken volcanic cone thrusts bizarrely from the azure sea. As you draw closer, you see that the lava octopus sends gnarled tentacles of flowing molten rock into the bubbling sea, surrounding the island with a thick, steamy mist.

Approaching the island, you see that even beneath the water there are molten cracks on the coastal floor.

Your small craft gets very hot as it draws closer to shore, and you are startled to see Swarny drop a small bird into the water which emerges completely boiled a few moments later.

As you sail to the far side of the Isle, you realize that this is perhaps the most inhospitable place on the planet. Volcanic gas rises from molten gashes in the treeless terrain, and fresh eruptions shake the air like a thunderstorm.

On the far side, the island is slightly more hospitable. You see living trees and, here and there, you catch sight of a black-sailed Slith ship wending its way through the mists and shiny, jagged rocks that surround the island.

By late afternoon, Swarny Pate lands the boat in a small, relatively hospitable inlet.

Go to Section 90.

# SECTION 100
# Giving Jewels to the Muckmonga

With no desire to fight the Muckmonga further, you toss your jewels to the ground and begin to flee. The creature, instead of taking your jewels as you thought he would, lets out a bubbling laugh which echoes through the nightmarish cave.

"I want no jewels . . . I crave blood!" it burbles.

If you have any healing tools or deadly weapons you had better use them since the demonic beast prepares to strike you dead.

**SAGARD (LEVEL 3: 1/1, 2/1, 3/2, 4/3)**
[20] [19] [18] [17] [16] [15] [14] [13] [12] [11] [10] [9] [8] [7] [6] [5] [4] [3] [2] [1] **(Begin the book again.)**

**MUCKMONGA (LEVEL 4: 1/1, 2/2, 3/3, 4/3)**
[19] [18] [17] [16] [15] [14] [13] [12] [11] [10] [9] [8] [7] [6] [5] [4] [3] [2] [1]

If you defeat the Muckmonga, go to Section 87. You may *not* flee.

# SECTION 101
# Treacherous Voyage

The stars glow like jewels in the death-black sky as Swarny Pate's boat sails through the murky sea. In time, when Suthorp's towers have sunk below the horizon, you make out islands silhouetted on the horizon. Most are composed of jutting rock and are probably uninhabited, but on some of them orange embers of dying fires glow.

In time, the soft rocking of the ship, the warm winds from the south, and the tranquil salt air make you drowsy. However, you know that falling asleep would be a sure invitation to be attacked by Swarny Pate and his two sinister Fexian shipmates.

Slowly, you slump over in your seat, feeling more tired than ever. Struggling to keep awake, you slit your finger on your gleaming blade, hoping that the sting will keep you awake. However, it doesn't.

Waking for just a moment when the ship lurches on a wave, you see the silhouettes of the two treacherous Fexian shipmates sneaking toward you, gleaming daggers in their hands. Knowing that you have no choice but to fight, you lunge with your sword. Your sudden flurry of activity catches them off balance, and you strike first.

**SAGARD (LEVEL 3: 1/1, 2/1, 3/2, 4/3)**
[20] [19] [18] [17] [16] [15] [14] [13] [12] [11] [10]
[9] [8] [7] [6] [5] [4] [3] [2] [1] (**Begin the book
again.**)

**FEXIAN SHIPMATES (LEVEL 3: 1/1, 2/1, 3/2,
4/3)**
   **SHIPMATE #1** [5] [4] [3] [2] [1]
   **SHIPMATE #2** [7] [6] [5] [4] [3] [2] [1]

If you have cut them down by the sixth round of
combat, go to Section 81; if not, they will be joined
by Swarny Pate. If he joins, he attacks first.

**SWARNY PATE (LEVEL 3: 1/1, 2/1, 3/2, 4/3)**
[7] [6] [5] [4] [3] [2] [1] (**He begs for mercy.**)

When you have defeated all of them, go to Section 81.
You may *not* flee the ship.

# SECTION 102
# Fighting Rules

Instructions always make things seem more complicated than they really are. If you have made it this far in the book, the fighting rules should be a snap. Basically, they are common sense. When in doubt about anything, consider what would really happen.

## BEFORE PLAYING

All you really need to play this game are this book and a pencil. Some players find that a four-sided die will make fighting quicker, but the random numbers on the page will generate the combat results perfectly well.

If you have gotten to this page, you know the basics of moving from one section to another. Now, all that is left to learn is how to *fight* and how to use the *status chart*.

# FIGHTING

In a number of places in this book, you will encounter enemies and choose to *(or have to)* fight them. There can be only three possible outcomes to a fight: you can *win, lose,* or *flee.*

*Winning a fight:* You win a fight when you have reduced an enemy's hit points to 0. Or, in situations when you are fighting more than one enemy, you win when you have reduced all of the enemies' hit points to 0.

*Losing a fight:* You lose a fight when your number of available hit points falls to 0.

*Fleeing a fight:* When you feel that you might lose a particular fight or that the fight isn't worth having, you may *try* to flee. Fleeing is a 50–50 proposition. If you flip the pages and get an even number, if you toss a coin and roll heads, or if you roll a die and get an even number, you have successfully fled.

You may attempt to flee only before your combat turn, and only once per round.

When you have fled successfully, read the "flee" section at the end of the combat page, and it will direct you to another page.

Be warned: Some adversaries are impossible to flee from. They are specially marked. If you fail to flee, continue the combat normally.

# HOW COMBAT WORKS

Combat takes place in rounds and is resolved by generating random numbers from 1 to 4. The tool for doing this is included in the book. Note that there is a number from 1 to 4 printed on the upper corner of each right-hand page. If you look away and flip randomly through the book, stopping before you get to the end, you will have a random number.

For combat, Sagard and his opponent (or opponents) take turns. Unless otherwise stated, *Sagard strikes first*. After he strikes, the opponent strikes. That completes one round of combat. Combat can go for several rounds and must end when Sagard wins, loses, or flees. When this happens, follow the instructions on that page. These will direct you to your next adventure.

Every battle you fight will be different. The difficulty of each battle will be determined by how many hit points your opponent has and what his fighting level is.

*Hit points* are the number of points of damage a player may take before he is out of the combat. As Sagard, you are given *20 hit points* in the beginning of the game. (This number will change in the course of the game, though in this book Sagard may not exceed 20 hit points.) That means you will have to take 20 points of damage before you are out of the game.

A typical battle sheet looks like this:

**SAGARD (LEVEL 3: 1/1, 2/1, 3/2, 4/3)**
[20] [19] [18] [17] [16] [15] [14] [13] [12] [11] [10]
[9] [8] [7] [6] [5] [4] [3] [2] [1] (You may fight no
more. Hobble to Section X.)

Each time you score a hit or hits on an opponent,
cross out the total number of boxes' worth of damage you do on his chart, like so:

**ORC (LEVEL 1: 1/0, 2/0, 3/1, 4/1)**
[12] [11] [10] [9] [8] [7] [6] [5] [4] [3] [2] [1] (You
have successfully defeated the Orc. Go to Section X.)

*Fighting levels,* as illustrated above, are different
for different characters. In this book, Sagard begins
as a Level 3 fighter. Fighting levels go from 0 to 5.
The higher the fighting level, the more dangerous
the opponent is. The important fighting information
is included in every melee so that you don't need to
refer to this chart except when you increase a level.

## FIGHTING LEVEL TABLE
### Flip/Die Roll

|         | 1 | 2 | 3 | 4 |
|---------|---|---|---|---|
| Level 0 | 0 | 0 | 0 | 1 |
| Level 1 | 0 | 0 | 1 | 1 |
| Level 2 | 0 | 1 | 1 | 2 |
| Level 3 | 1 | 1 | 2 | 3 |
| Level 4 | 1 | 2 | 3 | 3 |
| Level 5 | 2 | 3 | 3 | 4 |

These numbers refer to hit points or damage points. For instance, if Sagard, a Level 3 fighter, gets a 4, he does 3 hit points of damage to his opponent and crosses them off the enemy's chart. Likewise, if a Level 5 fighter gets a 1, he does 2 points of damage. Just to test yourself, what happens if a Level 3 fighter gets a 2?

If you said 1 point of damage, you are correct.

Therefore, the dangerousness of an opponent can be determined by looking at both his fighting level and the number of hit points he has.

Remember, there can only be three possible outcomes for any fight: win, lose, or flee. If your number drops to 0, read the section after the hit points and follow those instructions. Hit points are permanent, but Sagard will frequently rest or eat and regain points. Regained points will be clearly stated in the book.

Bear in mind that the number of Sagard's hit points will go up and down in the course of the game. Sagard carries damage from battle to battle. After each battle, mark Sagard's available hit points on Sagard's *status sheet* (explanation later). Do likewise when Sagard regains hit points.

# BONUSES

Along the way, you will pick up bonuses for your journey. These come in four forms: trophies, experience marks, weapons and armor, and special items. Each of these bonuses is valuable to you in a different way.

*Trophies* are valuable to the Ordeal of Courage. The more trophies Sagard has, the better the chance he will be accepted into the tribe.

*Experience marks* are permanent. Sagard will take them with him from book to book. The purpose of experience marks is to determine Sagard's fighting level. At the beginning of this book, Sagard is at Level 3. When he has 60 experience marks, he moves up to Level 4.

*Weapons and armor* are valuable for combat and will give Sagard an edge when fighting. The value of these weapons will be explained when the weapon is awarded.

*Special items* serve their own purposes. Some special items, such as shields, can be used to absorb hit points; others, such as magic potions, can be used to restore hit points when Sagard needs them.

Bonuses and combat results are recorded on the Sagard *status chart* below.

# SAGARD STATUS CHART

| Experience marks | Level | Trophies |
|---|---|---|
| | | _____ |
| | | _____ |
| | | _____ |
| **Current Hit Points** | | _____ |
| | | _____ |
| | | _____ |

| Weapons and Armor | Effect on Combat |
|---|---|
| _____ | _____ |
| _____ | _____ |
| _____ | _____ |
| _____ | _____ |
| **Special Items** | **Powers** |
| _____ | _____ |
| _____ | _____ |
| _____ | _____ |
| _____ | _____ |
| _____ | _____ |

Each time Sagard is involved in combat or regains hit points, update his *status sheet*. Sagard starts out with 20 hit points. Suppose he loses 8 of them—he is left with 12. Then, let us say he eats and regains 5 hit points in the next section; he now has 17 hit points. Next time you go into battle, remember how many hit points you have, and modify your *status sheet* accordingly. Remember, Sagard may never have more than 20 hit points.

Now that you've read the rules, get to it! Refer back if you have questions.

# CURRENT STATUS SHEET
## Conflict #

| | 1 | 2 | 3 | 4 | 5 | 6 | 7 | 8 | 9 | 10 |
|---|---|---|---|---|---|---|---|---|---|---|
| | 20 | 20 | 20 | 20 | 20 | 20 | 20 | 20 | 20 | 20 |
| S | 19 | 19 | 19 | 19 | 19 | 19 | 19 | 19 | 19 | 19 |
| A | 18 | 18 | 18 | 18 | 18 | 18 | 18 | 18 | 18 | 18 |
| G | 17 | 17 | 17 | 17 | 17 | 17 | 17 | 17 | 17 | 17 |
| A | 16 | 16 | 16 | 16 | 16 | 16 | 16 | 16 | 16 | 16 |
| R | 15 | 15 | 15 | 15 | 15 | 15 | 15 | 15 | 15 | 15 |
| D' | 14 | 14 | 14 | 14 | 14 | 14 | 14 | 14 | 14 | 14 |
| S | 13 | 13 | 13 | 13 | 13 | 13 | 13 | 13 | 13 | 13 |
| | 12 | 12 | 12 | 12 | 12 | 12 | 12 | 12 | 12 | 12 |
| H | 11 | 11 | 11 | 11 | 11 | 11 | 11 | 11 | 11 | 11 |
| I | 10 | 10 | 10 | 10 | 10 | 10 | 10 | 10 | 10 | 10 |
| T | 9 | 9 | 9 | 9 | 9 | 9 | 9 | 9 | 9 | 9 |
| | 8 | 8 | 8 | 8 | 8 | 8 | 8 | 8 | 8 | 8 |
| P | 7 | 7 | 7 | 7 | 7 | 7 | 7 | 7 | 7 | 7 |
| O | 6 | 6 | 6 | 6 | 6 | 6 | 6 | 6 | 6 | 6 |
| I | 5 | 5 | 5 | 5 | 5 | 5 | 5 | 5 | 5 | 5 |
| N | 4 | 4 | 4 | 4 | 4 | 4 | 4 | 4 | 4 | 4 |
| T | 3 | 3 | 3 | 3 | 3 | 3 | 3 | 3 | 3 | 3 |
| S | 2 | 2 | 2 | 2 | 2 | 2 | 2 | 2 | 2 | 2 |
| | 1 | 1 | 1 | 1 | 1 | 1 | 1 | 1 | 1 | 1 |
| | 0 | 0 | 0 | 0 | 0 | 0 | 0 | 0 | 0 | 0 |

# ABOUT THE AUTHORS

GARY GYGAX is the co-creator of the DUNGEONS & DRAGONS® Game, the wildly popular pursuit that took the country by storm six years ago. He is the Chairman of the Board and president of TSR, Inc., the company that produces it.

FLINT DILLE was part of George Lucas's development team for the "Star Wars" TV show. He has written scripts for various animated television series, including "G.I. Joe," "Mr. T," "Robo-Force," and "Transformers." Most recently, Mr. Dille story-edited the script for the *Transformers* movie.

# ABOUT THE ILLUSTRATOR

LESLIE MORRILL is an award-winning children's book illustrator who holds a Masters of Fine Arts from Cranbrook Academy in Bloomfield Hills, Michigan. He currently resides in Connecticut with his wife and daughter.

# SAGARD

## THE BARBARIAN GAMEBOOK™ Series

### by Gary Gygax and Flint Dille

**A new fantasy/adventure series
written by the co-creator of the
Dungeons & Dragons® game**

Enter the realm of Sagard—heroic warrior of the barbarian world—to challenge the seen and unseen forces of evil. You, the reader, become Sagard, and *only you* can fight the battles, make the choices and take the chances at each turn of the page.

## #1 THE ICE DRAGON

In accordance with age-old tribal customs, you must journey through the wilderness surrounding your village to prove that you are a warrior of great courage. Should you fail, you will be banished from your tribe forever. To be truly successful, you must return with the heart of THE ICE DRAGON.

Read on . . .

**THE BARBARIAN GAMEBOOK™ Series**

## #2 THE GREEN HYDRA

As the only survivor of a bloody ambush, you alone can save your homeland and tribe by taking part in the most dangerous adventure of your life. Along the way, you will encounter deadly enemies—the indestructible Smoke Demon; the hideous razor-clawed Nightripper; and the Slith Assassins, trained in the arts of death. These enemies prepare you to face the deadliest challenge of all—when you enter the tomb of THE GREEN HYDRA.

**Coming Soon . . .**

## #3 THE CRIMSON SEA

Named for all the blood that has been spilled upon its waters, THE CRIMSON SEA is filled with unspeakable horrors. But you must sail these waters to rescue the woman you love and to fulfill your destiny. Though you face countless dangers along the way, your greatest challenge comes at the end of your journey, when you battle the evil Sultoon, ruler of a wicked city of sorcery and black magic.

Read on . . .

## SAGARD
### THE BARBARIAN GAMEBOOK™ Series

### #4 THE FIRE DEMON

The lost City of Ivory, once a great kingdom, has fallen into the clutches of a demonic sorcerer. Only you, with your great strength and courage, can rescue the city. Your long and difficult quest takes you deep into the Dark Heart of the jungle to free the ancient city. Will you return alive? Or will you fall victim to The Curse of Ushad-I and be engulfed by the flames of THE FIRE DEMON?

### Look for SAGARD THE BARBARIAN Gamebook™ Series at your local bookstore!

**Archway Paperbacks, Published by Pocket Books**